NIALL'S BRIDE

HIGHLANDER FATE BOOK FOUR

STELLA KNIGHT

PRONUNCIATION GUIDE

Niall - NYEE-əl
Caitria - KAY-tria
Artair - AHR-tər
Drostan - DROST-an
Liusaidh - LYOO-si
Tadhg - TIE-G
Ferghas - FUR-gəs
Latharn - LA-urn
Muir - MYOU-er
Eithne - AYN-yuh
Ailsa - AIL-suh

CHAPTER 1

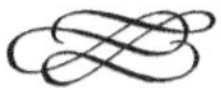

Edinburgh, Scotland
Present Day

"Time travel?"

Niall tried to keep his tone neutral as he said the two words, meeting the eyes of his friend, Scott Chapman.

Scott had summoned Niall to his office at the University of Edinburgh to confess why he had a sudden interest in medieval Scotland . . . in particular, the Highlands. It was because his sister Isabelle had traveled back in time to the year 1390, where she was now wed to a Highland laird.

Niall knew the proper response to this should be disbelief, shock, or even amusement. But he sat perfectly still, his expression a stoic mask. Scott had no idea that Niall was aware of the reality of time travel. *All too well,* he thought with a stab of bitterness.

Scott trained his blue eyes on Niall's face, his hands gripping the edge of his desk as if waiting for Niall to laugh, yell—or both.

"Jesus, Niall," Scott said finally, raking a hand through his dark hair and leaning back in his chair. "*Say* something. Tell me I'm crazy. Laugh. Threaten to toss me into the loony bin. Anything."

"Well," Niall said, allowing his mask of stoicism to crumble as he cracked a smile. "I'd have to commit myself to the 'loony bin' as well."

Scott's eyes widened, filling with surprise, then relief.

"So you believe me."

"Yes," Niall said. "But . . . I'm not sure you'll believe me."

Scott tensed, his eyebrows knitting together in a worried frown.

"We are talking about time travel," Scott said, expelling a breath. "I think suspension of disbelief is already on the table."

"Many members of my family are time travelers," Niall said. As he spoke the words, a tension he didn't know he possessed dissipated. It surprised him how good it felt to finally say the words out loud.

Scott's eyes grew increasingly wide as Niall told him all about the dark family secret—that he, his father, his grandfather before him, and many other family members all possessed the ability to travel through time. It was one of the reasons his father and grandfather had become such acclaimed historians; they'd gotten to see history firsthand.

"My father was obsessed with time travel," Niall continued. "He took many trips—some brief, some long—I think it took a toll on his body and hastened his death."

A stab of grief pierced him at the memory of his father, Ian O'Kean, who'd died a couple of years before. He'd never known his mother, who'd died of a long illness when he was still a baby. It had just been him and his father. Ian had parlayed his expertise of the European Dark Ages into best-selling books and high-paying speaking engagements. He'd been obsessed with traveling through time, and had taken many trips, which Niall believed contributed to his death at the relatively young age of fifty. The doctors had informed him a heart attack had killed him, but Ian had always been in good health.

Scott stumbled to his feet, raking his hand through his hair as he paced the small space of his office.

"You're a historian, too," he said, turning to face Niall with narrowed eyes. "All this time, have you been—"

"No," Niall swiftly interrupted. "I've never traveled through time, and I've never wanted to. I think it's dangerous, and there are too many ramifications. I've studied history the old-fashioned way—books and research."

His tone was more defensive than he intended,

but he prided himself on not cheating and using the same underhanded tricks his father had.

"OK. So . . . this time-travel thing," Scott muttered. "If it runs in families—how come my sister can travel through time and I can't?"

"It's not always genetic. Not every member of my family can time travel—and they should consider themselves lucky," Niall said, not bothering to hide the bitterness in his voice.

"You've never been curious? Never wanted to see for yourself what ancient Rome was like? The Victorian era?"

"Time travel is more complicated than that. For one thing, it's difficult to pinpoint the exact year you'll travel to. I've heard stories of relatives attempting to get to the sixteenth century—only to end up in the Viking era," Niall said with a sigh, rubbing his temples.

"I can't believe this. I mean—I do, but—*Jesus*. I ask you here to get this time-travel bombshell off my chest about Isabelle, and you hit me with something even more incredible," Scott said, sinking back into his chair. "I was half expecting you to end our friendship after I told you."

Niall frowned. Scott was an American professor from Chicago who'd come to Scotland to be with his Scottish wife and teach classics at the University of Edinburgh. As a native Scot, Niall rarely ventured to the States, and he'd never have met the American professor had their paths not crossed at a medieval classics conference in Edinburgh. He'd only known Scott for a couple of years, but he considered him a close friend. Even if he hadn't believed his story, he wouldn't have ended his friendship with Scott. Did he seem so rigid and closed off?

Niall had to conclude that he probably did. Having such a massive secret to hide had made him close himself off to people—friends and lovers alike. As a medieval historian, his work as a researcher and consultant for museums and publications afforded him the ability to immerse himself in old books and ancient documents rather than interact with other people, keeping them at a distance. Scott was one of the few—the only, he grudgingly admitted—close friends he had.

"Well, I'm glad you told me," he told Scott. "And to be honest, I'm glad to have someone outside my family know about time travel . . . and not think I'm crazy."

He hesitated, wondering if he should tell Scott about the dreams which had plagued him for months now, dreams of a beautiful auburn-haired woman in fourteenth-century clothing. At first, the dreams had only consisted of glimpses of her and then they became more vivid. He would see her approaching him with a wide smile, throwing her head back and laughing, dancing in his arms, and at times the dreams tilted toward the erotic—her lush body beneath his, his lips peppering kisses on her nude flesh.

Recently, the dreams had grown dark, showing

the woman in looming danger from an unknown threat. These dreams had become so pervasive that he was now convinced the woman in his dreams existed . . . and that she was in real danger.

"Niall?" Scott asked, pulling him from the maelstrom of his thoughts. "Are you all right?"

Niall hesitated for only a moment before he spoke.

"Speaking of time travel and the past . . . I've been having dreams. Dreams about a woman who I think is real."

Scott listened intently as Niall told him about the dreams, and the danger she seemed to be in.

"I had one the other night—the most vivid one I've ever had. When I woke up . . . I wanted to go to her. And given her clothing, I can only assume she's in the past. Going to her would mean traveling back in time—something I told myself I'd never do."

Scott offered him a sympathetic nod.

"I would give you advice . . . but I think you already know what to do."

Niall expelled a sigh. He'd hoped Scott would tell him it was foolish to go back in time to rescue a mysterious woman who may or may not exist from some unforeseen danger—all on the account of dreams.

There was a sharp knock on the door, and Scott stiffened, glancing at the time.

"I have a meeting with a student," Scott said, giving him an apologetic look. "But I have a feeling this conversation isn't over. Want to meet for lunch tomorrow?"

As Niall left Scott's office to head to the Museum of Scotland, where he was consulting on an exhibit about women in medieval times, he tried to put their conversation from his mind and enjoy the day. The museum was only a half-mile walk from the university, and he took his time, savoring the details of the street.

Edinburgh was an old city, with many buildings from the past still standing. The street he was walking down, Cowgate, had once been an old drover's route where farmers led their cattle to local markets for sale. A mix of modern and medieval buildings dotted the street, and he grinned at the sight of cow statues erected on one pub—a colorful ode to its past.

His thoughts returned, unbidden, to Scott's advice about the woman in his dreams. *You already know what to do.*

Niall's chest tightened at the thought of traveling through time. He'd lost count of how many times at conferences other historians had mused over how wonderful it would be to travel through time, the awe of seeing the past for themselves. Niall had always held his tongue, not telling them that time travel was very real, and they should be happy that they were in the relative safety of the present. He preferred the safety of the present and using good old-fashioned books to research the past.

He had no desire to return to a time of rampant disease and danger.

If you don't go, what happens to the mystery woman? a phantom voice whispered in his mind, a whisper he tried to ignore.

His thoughts still preoccupied him when he arrived at his office at the museum, where he gave his approval over items that were going on display in the exhibit: gowns, engraved hand mirrors, prayer books. He wondered if the mystery woman from his dreams, if she existed, used items like this in her day-to-day life.

"Are you going to the museum's benefit ball, Niall?"

Niall looked up, still lost in his thoughts. Maisie, one of the museum curators, had poked her head into his office. He stiffened; Maisie had been trying to set him up with her niece for weeks.

"No. I have plans that night," Niall lied. He disliked museum balls and galas, preferring to spend his evenings with a good biography or historical tome and a glass of well-aged whiskey. Scott liked to tease him that he acted more like an old man than one of only thirty-two.

"That's too bad," Maisie said, expelling a sigh. "My niece needs a date for the ball. I think you two would get along well."

Niall just gave her a forced, polite smile. He knew women found him attractive; he had his mother's wavy, chestnut hair and his father's cerulean-blue eyes and strong, angular features.

He'd had his fair share of casual lovers, but he'd not dated anyone since the dreams of the mystery woman began—and he had no desire to.

Maisie left him alone with a polite good night, and when he returned to his penthouse later, he felt more tired than usual, his conversation with Scott still weighing on his mind.

He made himself a quick dinner, taking in the penthouse that he'd inherited from his father. He'd purposefully designed it to have a modernistic feel, with its white walls and minimalist decor. No one would ever guess that a historian lived here.

When he crawled into bed, the familiar stirrings of dread tugged at him; he was uncertain of what his dreams would hold. He resisted sleep for as long as he could, but when sleep claimed him— he saw her.

She was running, her gown torn, tears streaming down her face. The figure she ran from was someone he couldn't make out.

"Niall!" she screamed, her lovely face contorted in terror. "Please! Please—help me—"

He awoke with a gasp, anxiety and fear roiling through him, his body shaking violently. Never had one of his dreams had such immediacy, such looming violence.

There could be no more delay; no more denial. His mystery woman needed his help. And she needed it now.

CHAPTER 2

1390
MacGreghor Castle

Caitria gazed out her window at the lands that stretched beyond MacGreghor Castle, lost in daydreams. Dozens of miles to the southeast lay Inverness. Farther south—Glasgow and Edinburgh. She imagined what it would be like to venture farther south, to London. And then to venture even farther, crossing the Channel to get to the great cities of the continent—Paris, Prague, Siena.

She'd never ventured far beyond the castle grounds, other than trips to the local villages. Her mind often wandered when she stood at the window in her chamber, imagining what the world beyond looked like, a world which her overprotective parents would never allow her to see.

"Caitria."

Caitria turned, pinning a smile on her face as her mother, Liusaidh, entered her chamber along with two young chambermaids, Ailsa and Eithne. They were all carrying gowns; her mother met her eyes and smiled.

"What are ye doing standing by the window in yer underdress? The season's changing; we cannae have ye falling ill."

Liusaidh gestured to Ailsa, who hurried to the window and closed it. Caitria ignored the stab of resentment that pierced her, moving away from the window.

"We need tae get ye prepared for the betrothal feast; ye've been in need of new gowns. What do ye think of these? I personally chose a dressmaker all the way from Edinburgh."

Ailsa and Eithne helped her mother lay the gowns down on the bed, and Caitria studied them dispassionately. They were lovely gowns: one a deep sapphire blue, the other a green that matched her eyes, but Caitria had to feign enthusiasm. How many lovely gowns had her mother dressed her in over the years? They all looked the same to her.

"They're both lovely, Mother," she said. "Either one is fine with me."

"The green," Liusaidh said, beaming down at the dress. "Shows off yer lovely eyes. And I think Artair will like ye in it."

"Yes," Caitria agreed, though she felt nothing at the thought of pleasing Artair, the man she was to marry.

"Why doonae ye try it on? Ailsa, Eithne—help my daughter."

Caitria kept her smile pinned on her face, hoping she looked sufficiently excited as her mother and the chambermaids fussed over her, helping her change into the green gown. She walked over to the mirror after they'd dressed her, taking herself in.

Though she was twenty-five, her green eyes sparkling with youth, the green gown bringing out their color, she felt much older. She lifted up her long wavy auburn hair to take in the finely cut bodice, forcing herself to smile at her reflection. She looked like the respectful eldest daughter of a powerful clan laird. She might as well have been a lovely ornament.

"'Tis lovely," she repeated, her face becoming strained from the smile she wore. Caitria had her part to play, and she played it well.

Her mother clucked in delight, dismissing the two maids with a wave, and moved to stand at her side.

Caitria took in her mother's reflection. She'd inherited her looks from her mother—they had the same shade of auburn hair, the same green eyes, the same high cheekbones and fine-boned features. Her mother was in her mid forties and still possessed a youthful vivacity. When her father wasn't looking, she'd noticed some clan nobles casting surreptitious glances her mother's way.

"Ah, just think of it, my Caitria," Liusaidh said, her smile wide. "Soon ye'll be a married woman."

Dread swirled in Caitria's gut, and it took great effort to not let her smile falter. As the lone daughter of the chieftain of the MacGreghor clan, Caitria's hand in marriage had been a highly sought after one, given how much land her father controlled. Whoever married Caitria gained control of those lands once her father died or stepped down as chieftain.

The man her father had chosen for her, Laird Artair Dalaigh, was handsome and polite, yet she felt nothing for him. Though he treated her with kindness, she sensed a similar disinterest from him. Like most of her suitors, she knew he was wedding her for her father's lands, though given the rumors she'd heard about him, she wondered why he was bothering to marry at all. Artair had his own manor and patch of land in the north where they would live after they wed. He was only loosely affiliated with the clan he'd been born into, and would officially join Clan MacGreghor after they wed. He was coming to the castle at her father's invitation for the few weeks leading up to their wedding to spend more time with her and the nobles of the clan. After the wedding, they'd return to his manor.

I'll go from one castle tae another, Caitria thought, a heaviness seeping into her bones. Not to the faraway lands she'd always dreamed of visiting, not to the freedom she secretly craved.

"Caitria?" Liusaidh asked, noticing the sudden darkness of her expression. She frowned with concern. "Are ye all right?"

Caitria hesitated. She'd only once expressed her desire to travel to her mother and was swiftly chastised.

"Ye are the lone child and heir of Drostan MacGreghor," Liusaidh had breathed, her face hot with anger. "Yer duty is tae yer family, yer clan, and these lands. Ye're our only surviving heir. Ye'll marry and sire sons tae continue the MacGreghor name. I'll hear no more of this desire tae travel—and doonae think tae express such wishes tae yer father—ye'll give him a fright. Travel is dangerous for lasses of high birth."

Caitria's mouth tightened at the memory. It was one of the few times her mother had raised her voice in anger to her.

Caitria knew how much Liusaidh loved her, how much both her parents loved her. She'd lost her older brother Tadhg the previous year during a hunting accident. Her parents had been overprotective of her before, but ever since his death, their protectiveness had become stifling. But to disobey their wishes and seek the freedom she craved would mean turning her back on them—and breaking their already fragile hearts. Instead, Caitria had buried her true desires deep and feigned excitement and gratitude when her father informed her she would wed Laird Dalaigh.

"I'm fine," she lied, forcing yet another smile. "I'm just nervous about the betrothal feast."

"All will be well," Liusaidh said, reaching down to squeeze Caitria's hand. "Ye'll look lovely in yer gown, and all the guests will be happy tae celebrate yer union with Artair."

"My lady, the cook has a question for ye in the kitchens," Ailsa said, poking her head into the chamber with an apologetic look.

"I'll be right there," Liusaidh said, turning back to face Caitria. "I should have ye come with me— ye'll need tae learn how tae manage a castle's servants . . . but I'll allow ye tae rest. Ye have an important night tomorrow."

Relief filled Caitria; the last thing she wanted to do was spend her afternoon at her mother's side as she trained her to become just like her, the wife of a laird whose duties consisted of birthing sons and ordering servants around.

As soon as her mother left, Caitria changed out of the confining gown and into a more comfortable gown she wore for riding. She needed to get out of this stifling chamber. She threw a cloak around her head to cover herself and slipped out of the chamber, keeping her head ducked low as she made her way out of the castle, exiting through its rear. Her parents—especially her father—didn't like it when she left the castle grounds without a guard, but she had no desire to have a hovering presence trail her when she just needed air.

She was afraid someone would spot her, but the servants were deep in their preparations for the massive betrothal feast that was taking place the next evening, and no one paid her any mind. Her tension dissipated as soon as she slipped past the open castle gates, making her way to the thick patch of forest that lay just beyond the castle.

Caitria lowered her cloak, inhaling the cool air scented with fragrant fall leaves and damp earth, until she reached her favorite clearing. She tossed aside her cloak and lifted her gown, slipping out of her shoes to dip her toes into the stream that meandered through the clearing. She wondered idly what the ocean looked like and closed her eyes, picturing herself climbing onto her favorite horse, Kerr, and riding to the ocean. And then after that, to some unknown destination. Her smile widened at just the thought.

"What has ye smiling so, lass?"

Caitria stiffened at the familiar voice. She removed her feet from the stream and turned.

One of the clan nobles, Ferghas, stood several yards behind her, leaning against a tree with a flirtatious smile. Ferghas had been the top contender for her hand before her father chose Artair. While he was handsome, affable, and well liked, there was something about him that made her skin crawl. She preferred the distant Artair over him.

Unease swirled through her veins as he stepped closer. How had he known she was here? Had he followed her?

"Just thinking of the betrothal feast," she lied, and took pleasure in how his smile fell. "I should get back tae the castle."

"Please allow me tae escort ye," he said, stepping forward to take her arm, linking it with his before she could reply.

She gritted her teeth and walked along with him, as he continued, "I must confess my disappointment that yer father chose Laird Dalaigh over me for yer hand. Ye ken I've always cared for ye, lass."

Caitria had known Ferghas for years through the gatherings her father held at the castle, and she'd noticed him watching her. But he'd watched her with a dark predatory gleam in his eyes, like that of a wolf stalking his prey, and it chilled her to the bone.

"I'm sure ye'll wed a lass who'll make ye happy," she returned, now regretting the decision to leave behind her guard.

He stopped walking and turned her to face him, his dark eyes intense as they probed hers.

"Ye're the only woman who'll make me happy, Caitria."

Caitria swallowed, unease rippling through her.

"I'm betrothed tae Artair."

"That boring man cannae make ye happy, Caitria," he insisted. "I can."

"The decision has already been made," she said, as his grip tightened on her arm, uncomfortably so. "Please—let me go."

But Ferghas's hold only tightened, and tendrils of pain coiled through her as his eyes darkened.

"My lady."

Caitria whirled, and Ferghas released her. Relief coursed through her at the sight of her chief guard, Hendry.

"Hendry," Ferghas said, beaming. Gone was the man who seconds before brimmed with danger, and in his place the affable man everyone in the clan adored. "I'm glad tae see ye. I was just escorting the lady back tae the castle."

Hendry still looked suspicious, though he gave him a nod.

"I'll escort the lady back, as is my duty," Hendry said.

Caitria scrambled away from Ferghas, giving Hendry a grateful nod.

They headed back to the castle, and when Caitria glanced back at Ferghas, his polite smile had vanished, and there was no mistaking the darkness in his eyes.

CHAPTER 3

Inverness, Scotland
Present Day

"I think this is going to be a part of my new job description. Helping people travel through time," Scott said, offering Niall a wide grin.

Niall returned his smile, shooting him a brief, wry glance as he maneuvered his car through the streets of Inverness.

After his latest nightmare about the mystery woman, he'd been unable to sleep—and he knew what he had to do. He'd called Scott, who'd picked up on the first ring.

"I can't live with myself if there really is someone out there who needs my help," Niall had said. "I . . . I need to go to her."

A pause had settled in on the other end of the line, and Niall had feared Scott would admonish him.

21

"Well, then. Let's get you out of the twenty-first century," Scott had replied, to his great relief.

They'd taken the train from Edinburgh to Inverness earlier that day. Niall had planned for an extended absence before his departure, informing the museum and his work contacts that he needed to leave the country to deal with a family emergency.

He and Scott were now headed to vintage and antique stores for Niall to collect the final items he'd need before his journey. Thanks to his father and grandfather, he already had a medieval outfit— a tunic and breeches, and even English and Scottish coins from the fourteenth century. A medical contact of his father's had given him tablets of penicillin, thankfully not asking too many questions when Niall collected them before his departure from Edinburgh.

He was able to put his belongings into a pocket his father had sown into the sleeve of the medieval tunic, as the only way of bringing things from the future to the past was to have them on your person, and even then, such items weren't guaranteed to survive the journey.

He could have undertaken these final errands on his own, but he needed Scott for moral support. Though his family were well-worn time travelers, this was his first venture to the past, and Scott had seen his sister Isabelle safely off to the fourteenth century. Besides, he figured Scott's presence would prevent him from mulling too much over the sheer insanity of what he was doing—traveling back through time on account of dreams.

But they're more than dreams, he told himself. His gut instinct told him that this woman was real; she was in danger, and for whatever reason, he was the only one who could help her.

"How do you know exactly where to go?" Scott was asking, as they pulled into the parking lot of a vintage weapons store. "How do you know you won't end up in prehistoric Scotland? Renaissance Italy? Ancient Mexico?"

"This is going to sound crazy," Niall said after a brief pause, and Scott barked out a laugh.

"My friend. We are beyond sounding crazy at this point."

"I think—because I'm having dreams about this woman—I'll be sent right to her once I go through the portal."

It was hard for him to admit this out loud. Even though he knew the reality of time travel, his rational mind refused to go beyond that—to the notion of fate tying him to some unknown woman in the past. But there was a reason he was having the dreams, a reason they were so real and vivid to him.

He wondered if the *stiuireadh* had something to do with his dreams. The stiuireadh were descendants of druid witches who assisted travelers through time. But his family was capable of traveling through time on their own without assistance.

He suspected the cause of his dreams would remain a mystery.

"So, what's your backstory?" Scott asked moments later, after they'd left the vintage weapons store with a dagger that Niall could stow beneath his tunic. "I'm sure the people of the past will be curious about a man with a modern Scottish brogue suddenly showing up in their midst."

"I'm a traveling wine merchant making my way through the Highlands on my way to the Low Countries," he replied.

He'd decided on this backstory once he knew he was traveling to the past; he could pretend to do business in a nearby village while he tried to get close to the woman to figure out what danger she was in. Given her clothing, she was likely highborn, and he figured a wine merchant would have relatively easy access to a castle—and she did live in a castle, according to the images in his dreams.

Scott nodded his approval and gave him a sly grin.

"One thing I've failed to ask you. Is this mystery woman 'bonnie'?" Scott asked, switching from his American accent to Niall's Scottish one.

"That's not what this is about," Niall said with a scowl, though a sliver of heat crept through him at the memory of the woman's beauty. "I just want to help her if I can. I'm hoping that when I find her— if I find her—she's perfectly fine, and I can return in less than a week or so. And then my life can go back to normal without those pesky dreams."

His tone left no room for argument, and Scott didn't pursue this topic of conversation further. His playful expression faded as they slid back into the car.

"If you happen to arrive in the same year as my sister . . . "

Scott looked uncharacteristically shy as he slid a letter out of his pocket and handed it to him. Niall took the letter, giving his friend an understanding smile as he slipped it into his pocket.

Scott gave him a nod of thanks, his vulnerability plain. Though Scott was a jokester and tried to keep things lighthearted, Niall knew how much he missed his sister.

"I need a brief break from time-travel talk," Niall said, starting up the car. They'd only discussed his upcoming time travel during the journey from Edinburgh and as they ran errands. "Tell me what's going on in the world of Scott Chapman."

As Scott told him about his new class of students and their prowess in the subject of classics, Niall listened and tried to absorb his surroundings as he drove—his modern, twenty-first century surroundings. The cars that clogged the streets, passersby on their cell phones, a plane flying above in the distance. All the comforts of modernity—and he was leaving it all behind.

Temporarily, he told himself. This little mission would be temporary, and once he returned, he had no intention of going to the past again.

He slowed his car down at a stop sign, and casually glanced to his left, where Old High Church stood. Gazing at it, a sudden and powerful wave of déjà vu seized him. He'd visited Inverness and the church—one of the city's prime historical sites—many times, but this was a different sort of déjà vu. The sense that he had and had not yet been here before—which made no sense.

"You could at least pretend to listen," Scott said, his lips twitching with an amused smile. "I just said I'm going to fly to Mars tomorrow, and you nodded."

"Sorry," Niall said apologetically, shaking his head as if to rid himself of the odd sense of déjà vu. He considered telling Scott what he'd just experienced, but he didn't know how to explain the sensation. He swallowed, turning his focus back to the road. "I'm just nervous about tomorrow."

"I would be, too," Scott said, giving him a look of understanding and sympathy. "But I'm glad you're doing it."

When Niall returned to the hotel room he'd booked for the night, dread swirled through his gut. What had that sense of déjà vu been about? Was it some instinctive warning?

And what if he couldn't time travel after all? Or what if he could, and it went horribly wrong, and he died during the journey? Such occurrences were rare, but his father had spoken of relatives who'd attempted to travel—only their bodies couldn't handle the journey and they didn't survive.

But he had to admit to himself that he was the most worried about his journey through time succeeding. Fourteenth-century Scotland wasn't necessarily the most peaceful time for his country; there was rampant clan warfare, battles with the English, and a little thing called the Black Plague, which struck Scotland in the earlier part of the century.

Niall set aside his fear with great effort, taking a deep breath as he closed his eyes. He had no choice; he knew that if he didn't go, the dreams would continue to plague him. He just needed to get this over with so he could get his life back.

He didn't dream of the woman that night, his sleep black and empty, but this didn't bring him relief. It chilled him to the bone, and he woke up with a cold unease. What if he was already too late?

"What happened?" Scott asked, taking in Niall's pale face as they slid into their rental car the next morning. "Another nightmare?"

"I just didn't sleep well," Niall said, not wanting to voice out loud his fear that he was already too late to rescue the mystery woman.

"Well, you look the part," Scott said, his eyes roaming over Niall.

Niall wore a white tunic and a pair of breeches. He'd gotten some curious looks as he'd checked out of his room, with the clerk asking him if he was attending a medieval festival.

Scott had offered to take over the driving to get them to Tairseach, for which Niall was grateful.

His stomach churned with nervous anticipation during the entire drive, which rose to a crescendo by the time they arrived at Tairseach.

Niall took in the ruins of the ancient village, a village that had once been home to druids who'd mysteriously disappeared. He'd been here several times before with his father, watching as he disappeared amid a vortex of wind. There were portal villages like Tairseach all over the world, but this was the one the Scottish branch of his family used to travel through time.

Though Niall had come here before, anxiety still spiraled through him as he stepped out of the car. He'd always found Tairseach unsettling, but he supposed it should be. It was a preternatural place, a portal that transported people through time and space.

He turned to glance back at Scott, who was leaning against the side of the car. As someone without the ability to travel, Niall knew that Scott couldn't see Tairseach—he could only see a wide expansive field.

"This is so . . . weird. I just dropped my sister off here only weeks ago," Scott said, shaking his head with a sigh.

"Unlike your sister, I have every intention of returning," Niall said firmly. He stepped forward to give Scott a brief embrace. "Thanks. For everything."

"It was my pleasure," Scott said, returning

Niall's embrace before stepping back. "I hope you find your girl."

Niall wanted to correct Scott—the mystery woman wasn't "his girl." She was just someone he wanted to help if he could.

But he just gave his friend one last smile before turning and approaching Tairseach.

He looked around, his gaze landing on the crumbling castle that lay at the edge of the village. His father always went to the ruins of the castle when he traveled, but he'd told Niall that one could travel from anywhere in the village. *You just follow the wind*, his father had said, as if traveling through time was just a matter of stepping onto an elevator and pressing a button.

Yet . . . he did feel and see the wind. At first it was light, only slightly ruffling the grass, and then it picked up in intensity. It came from the center of the village, yards away from the castle.

He turned to see if Scott had noticed anything amiss, but he was still leaning against the car, arms folded, the wind not affecting him at all. Scott gave him a puzzled smile. Niall gave him a brief nod before turning away, moving toward the vortex. *Just follow the wind.*

His heart picked up its pace as he approached. His father had told him traveling through time was like riding a high-speed rollercoaster, or falling from a great height.

Niall hesitated, but only for a moment. In his

mind's eye, he saw the woman's wide-eyed panic, his name on her lips as she cried for help.

Determination erased his hesitance, and he stepped forward, allowing the wind to suck him forward—to an unknown past.

CHAPTER 4

1390
MacGreghor Castle

Niall didn't know exactly *where* he'd land once he traveled through time. His father had told him he'd ended up in the middle of forests, in privy chambers—and once he'd ended up in the center of a shallow lake.

When the world righted itself around him again, Niall found himself hunched over and clutching his knees on the ground, gasping for breath.

High-speed rollercoaster? He felt like he'd just fallen out of a plane and plummeted to the earth in free fall. Nausea twisted his stomach, and he took several deep breaths before stumbling to his feet.

He stood on the edge of the grounds of a sprawling stone castle, its front gates lit by torches.

31

Some event was taking place; carriages and horses streamed in through its open gates.

He froze. *Horses and carriages.* There'd been a part of him that feared he'd still find himself in present-day Scotland. But as he took in the horses, carriages, and medieval clothing of the people he could make out from this distance, he realized that he was indeed in the past.

But what year? He squinted at the riders and the carriages. By the style of clothing and the carriages, he estimated late fourteenth or early fifteenth century.

"My laird? What are ye doing out here?"

Niall whirled to find a man standing behind him, his eyebrows knitted together in a confused frown. He looked to be in his early twenties, with warm brown eyes and dark hair. He wore a dark tunic and belted plaid kilt—well, what was the precursor to the kilt, though it looked close enough. Niall instantly recognized the distinctive Scottish brogue. He'd recognize the Highland accent anywhere, even one that differed slightly from the modern one. A sense of relief filled him. By the man's clothing and accent, he knew he was in the Scottish Highlands. He'd just have to make his accent match the others around him as best he could.

"My laird?" the man repeated. "How did ye get out here? And why did ye change yer clothes? Ye're the guest of honor."

Niall stilled, his heart thundering in his chest.

Of all the scenarios he'd envisioned, this hadn't been one of them. His mind raced as he thought about what to do until he recalled something his father once told him about time travel.

"When all else fails, son," Ian O'Kean had said, his eyes twinkling. "Improvise."

"I lost my way," Niall said, hoping that he pulled off the accent. "And—these clothes suited me better."

The man stiffened, his eyes raking over him from head to toe. *Did I pull it off?* Niall wondered with panic. *Or can he tell I'm an intruder?*

But the man gave him a brief nod.

"The guests are arriving . . . the feast will start soon," the man said, turning to head toward the castle.

Niall assumed he was supposed to follow, and trailed after the man, taking deep breaths to quell his panic. The man led him past the gates, through a bustling courtyard and past the grand double doors of the castle.

The historian in Niall wanted to stop in his tracks and gawk. He'd been in many castles all over Scotland and England, but in his time, most were decrepit ruins of what they'd once been. This castle was vibrant and full of life. Candlelight and torches lit the interior, dominated by high-arched ceilings and stone floors; the pungent scent of roasting meats and vegetables wafted into the large corridor from the kitchens, which was abuzz with the conversations of the many guests who made their way toward the great hall.

He had to force himself to keep following the man, to school his expression to one of neutrality, as the man led him into the great hall.

"There she is," the man said, with a smile that was almost teasing, gesturing at the head table. "Yer betrothed."

My betrothed? Fear tore through him as he followed the man's gaze, and his heart plummeted in his chest.

It was *her*. The woman he'd been dreaming of. And she was even more beautiful in person.

Long auburn waves framed her heart-shaped face. She had deep-set green eyes, delicate, feminine features, and she wore a gown of emerald green that enhanced the color of her eyes. He could detect the luscious swell of her breasts beneath the bodice of her gown, and he swallowed, his desire stirring like a sleeping dragon coming awake.

She was absently sipping a cup of ale, her gaze trained on the table before her, but she stiffened, as if sensing his eyes on her. Her eyes locked with his, and a faint, lovely flush spread across her cheeks. Arousal spread through Niall at the sight, and his mouth went dry. She was the loveliest woman he'd ever seen.

"My laird? Artair?"

Niall tore his eyes away from the beauty, realizing that the man at his side was addressing him.

Artair. That was who this man thought he was. He'd just have to play along—for now.

"Are ye going tae stand there staring at the lass like ye're about tae bed her, or are ye going tae take yer seat at her side?" the man asked, his eyes shining with amusement.

"Aye," he forced himself to say, past dry lips.

He made his way past the milling guests and across the hall, his eyes still trained on hers, and for a precious few seconds it was like they were the only two people in the great hall.

"Artair!" a male voice boomed, and Niall halted as a tall, broad-shouldered man with kind, brown eyes and dark hair shot through liberally with gray intercepted him. "Tis good tae see ye! Ye spend much time holed up in yer manor in the north. I'm glad ye're tae spend some time here at the castle. We've got yer guest chamber all set up. I look forward tae spending time with my future son-in-law."

Son-in-law. This must be the beauty's father. Niall forced himself to nod. The man's grin widened as he turned to slide a glance toward his daughter.

"If ye weren't betrothed tae wed my Caitria, I'd have tae put my sword through ye for the way ye're looking at her," the man playfully threatened, with a good-natured chuckle. "But I'll not keep ye. Go tae yer future wife. But see me later; we have matters tae discuss."

To Niall's relief, the man left him alone, though

dread filled him at the thought of discussing "matters."

He continued to make his way toward the beauty—Caitria. *Caitria.* The woman who had come to him in his dreams, time and time again.

He reached her table and took the empty seat next to her that he assumed was meant for him. Her scent instantly struck him—lavender and rose-water. Another wave of desire washed over him as he met her gaze. She was even lovelier up close: her mouth wide and generous, her green eyes reminding him of shining jade stones. He tried to not let his gaze drift down the long, delicate arch of her throat to the curve of her breasts. He was reminded of one of the more erotic dreams he'd had about her, and his cock swelled against the fabric of his breeches.

He swallowed as she gave him a polite smile. He hadn't counted on her physical presence affecting him so much. And for all his planning, he hadn't decided on what he'd say to her when he met her. He thought he'd have more time to prepare; he hadn't counted on crossing her path so soon.

"Father tells me ye're staying here at the castle till we're wed," she said. Her voice was soft, her brogue almost musical; it wrapped around him like a warm summer's breeze.

"Aye," he forced himself to say, and cursed himself. He'd need to say something other than "aye" or people would get suspicious. But he didn't know much about this Artair person, other than her father seemed to like him, and they were to soon wed.

Caitria studied him, as if waiting for him to say more, so he continued, "I—I look forward tae the time I have here."

Caitria's eyes narrowed for a moment, and he wondered with nervousness if she was reacting to the sound of his voice; he guessed it differed fractionally from the actual Artair's. But she gave him a polite smile and nod.

"It . . . it will be good for us tae spend some time together, my laird. I look forward tae furthering our acquaintance," she said, lowering her eyes.

By the way she spoke to him, as if he were a polite stranger, he guessed that their—her and this Artair's—pending marriage—was one of convenience. She also looked perfectly miserable, he noticed now, though she tried to hide it behind her polite smile, and he felt an ache of sympathy for her. Niall had the sudden urge to do what he could to lift her veil of sadness. Women of this time had no choice in their lives—and often about whom they wed, if they were highborn—something else he hated about the past.

He was relieved that he didn't have to respond, as servants began to mill around the great hall, serving meals to the guests: roasted geese, bread, ale, and wine.

"Guests," Caitria's father bellowed from the opposite end of their long table, getting to his feet.

"We've all gathered here tae celebrate the joining of my daughter's hand in marriage to Laird Artair Dalaigh."

Laird Artair Dalaigh. He scanned his memory for the name. Given that people were mistaking him for Artair, he had to be a distant relative—but the name was not at all familiar.

The guests cheered as all eyes fell on him and Caitria. Caitria gave him a smile that looked a little pained, and Niall forced himself to smile as well. He had to stop focusing so much on her, and focus on what was being said. If everyone thought he was Laird Artair Dalaigh, he needed to know as much about him as possible.

"My bonnie daughter had many suitors, but I chose Laird Dalaigh as he's from a good family with lands of his own. I also ken him tae be a good man who will treat my Caitria the way she deserves," the man continued, looking at him with such genuine affection that a stab of guilt pierced Niall for his inadvertent deception. "I hope that ye will have many sons and continue the MacGreghor name."

The guests cheered, and dread scorched Niall's veins as Caitria's father gestured for him to stand. He wanted him to make a speech.

Improvise, he told himself sharply. *Just improvise. And keep it brief.*

Niall got to his feet, raising his cup of ale.

"I look forward tae my union with yer daughter," Niall said. He wondered just how closely his voice matched the actual Artair's. It must have been close enough, because most of the guests didn't look suspicious, merely waiting for him to finish his speech. He raised his cup and bellowed, "To the MacGreghor clan!"

That must have been the right thing to say, as the guests cheered and shouted their congratulations.

He sat back down as the feast began in earnest, turning his attention back to Caitria. He noticed that even the way she ate seemed practiced and rehearsed—she ate with delicate bites, placing down her spoon after each one, her eyes demurely downcast.

"How—how are ye this fine evening, lass?" he asked.

Her eyes flew to his, and he realized with dismay it surprised her that he was even addressing her. *This Artair is an arsehole,* he decided. He must barely give this lovely woman the time of day.

"Very well, my laird," she said, her tone stiff and formal. "I'm honored that my father chose tae honor our betrothal with this feast."

Was she always so rehearsed? He studied her for a moment, before he said, "Please, call me Ni—Artair," he amended quickly.

"Aye," she murmured, lowering her gaze. "Artair."

He wanted to converse with her more—at least to bring her out of her rehearsed shell—but

Caitria's father got to his feet, his eyes straying to him and Caitria.

"Will Laird Dalaigh and my Caitria honor the guests with a dance?"

Niall froze, but Caitria dutifully got to her feet, and Niall had no choice but to follow. All eyes were on them as they moved to the center of the hall.

Niall mentally ran through the dances of this time period, panicked, and finally settled on the quadrille, a dance performed all throughout Europe during medieval times. He'd only performed the quadrille once, during a medieval festival he'd attended several years before, and he prayed that the real Artair wasn't an excellent dancer.

To his relief, Caitria followed right along with the dance as he took her hand. He drew her body briefly against his before she drifted away, and electricity sparked through him at the feel of her lush body.

As they danced, both his anxiety and the other guests faded away. He couldn't take his eyes off her, relishing in the brief touches of her skin against his, the pretty flush that stained her cheeks whenever her eyes met his. When he pulled her close, he could feel her heart beat in tandem with his own, and as the chords of the music faded, they ended their dance enfolded in each other's arms.

Their eyes met, and he thought he saw her veil of politeness fade, and a flicker—just a flicker—of desire shining in her eyes. His eyes dropped to her lips, and he wanted nothing more than to seize them with his own, to press her lovely body close to his, to—

"Leave some of it to the marital bed!" a jovial voice boomed, and Niall stepped back abruptly, as if remembering where he was, while the guests all laughed and shouted their approval.

Caitria stumbled back from him, her face flushed, and Niall looked up to see her father get to his feet. He looked pleased at their closeness, giving Niall a nod, and gestured for the other guests to dance as well.

Heart hammering, Niall started to reach for Caitria's hand to escort her back to their table, but she stepped back out of his grasp.

"I'm—I'm sorry, my laird—Artair," she corrected herself hastily. "I—I'm not feeling well. I need tae take my leave."

He watched as she left the great hall, his heart thundering in his chest. Of everything he'd planned for when he came to the past, he hadn't counted on his instant and overwhelming attraction to the woman who'd drawn him here.

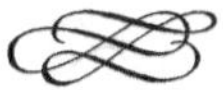

CHAPTER 5

*C*aitria darted out of the great hall, her heart racing. She'd never had such a visceral reaction to any man before—including Artair.

From the moment he'd entered the great hall, his eyes intently trained on hers, Caitria had been unable to breathe. She'd had to force herself to pretend not to notice his eyes on her, though his gaze left a blazing trail of heat on every inch of her skin. When he'd held her in his arms as they danced, arousal had careened throughout her body, and she had to concentrate on each step. At the end of their dance, time had seemed suspended, and she'd hoped—wished, ached—for him to kiss her. She had to flee from the great hall, even though she knew it displeased her parents, because she didn't think she could continue to act nonchalant around him.

When Caitria entered her chamber, she

dismissed the gossiping maids, sinking down onto the edge of her bed.

There was something . . . different about Artair tonight. Something she couldn't quite place. She'd always noticed that Artair was a handsome man, with chestnut-colored hair, sky-blue eyes, and strong, angular features—but he'd never caused such desire to spiral in her belly. She'd sensed the difference in just the way he looked at her. He'd never looked at her with such raw desire, just with a polite friendliness. He'd certainly never seemed interested in how she was doing, nor studied her as if trying to discern what was happening in her very soul.

But it was Artair. So what had changed? His voice was slightly different—deeper, the lilt of his words slightly off kilter. Other than the way he looked at her, *noticed* her, she couldn't pinpoint what else had changed.

None of this matters, she told herself, as she disrobed and crawled into bed. *Ye're marrying him either way. Perhaps this sudden desire will make everything easier . . . or it will simply fade.*

HER MOTHER SENT a maid to fetch her for midmorning supper, and dread coiled in her gut at the summons. She was in for a scolding for fleeing the betrothal feast the night before.

Yet when she entered her mother's private

chamber, it surprised her to find Liusaidh . . . smiling.

Liusaidh beamed, getting to her feet and crossing the chamber to take Caitria's hands.

"Ye and Artair were perfect together last night. Everyone could see how much desire there was between ye. I thought he'd take ye right there in the hall."

"Mother!" Caitria hissed, her face flaming, but her mother was already continuing.

"I admit . . . I felt some guilt over arranging for ye tae marry Artair. He's a perfectly kind man, but . . . distant. Ye always acted like strangers around each other. But last night, I was counting the bairns ye're going tae have."

"*Mother*," Caitria repeated, "I'd rather not discuss—"

"Ye'll be a married woman soon; we should discuss such matters," Liusaidh interrupted. "And given the way yer betrothed was looking at ye last night, ye'll soon be with child."

She waved for her to sit, and Caitria obliged, her face still warm, as her mother continued, "That's why I wanted tae share a meal with ye, in private. I ken I should have discussed such matters with ye the day ye became betrothed tae Artair, so 'tis far past time. For yer wedding night—"

"'Tis not necessary," Caitria interrupted, but Liusaidh continued, detailing exactly what she could expect during her wedding night.

Mortification filled her, and she ignored her

mother's words, her thoughts turning inward, though treacherous thoughts circled her mind with scandalous images of what her wedding night with Artair would be like. Until last night, she couldn't imagine it. But now she could picture his lips on hers, trailing down to her throat, even lower, to the swell of her breasts . . .

"Ah, I see ye're already thinking of it," Liusaidh was saying, a look of delight filling her green eyes. "I'm so happy with this match. Ye'll make a wonderful wife and mother."

Caitria's scandalous thoughts of Artair faded, and the familiar dread returned as she thought of the life that stretched before her—matron of a distant castle, just like her mother, never to see the faraway lands she desired to see. Her newfound desire for her betrothed hadn't made her longing for travel to disappear.

"Aye," Caitria murmured, focusing on her food as Liusaidh thankfully switched topics from her looming wedding night to more details of last night's feast—the guests who'd arrived, some minor altercation her father had gotten into with a clan noble, and the gossip she'd exchanged with another noble's wife.

Caitria was relieved when the meal came to an end, and her mother pecked her on the cheek and sent her on her way. She was still disconcerted from her reaction to Artair last night and needed time to herself.

When she reached her chamber, she halted in

her tracks. Artair stood outside her chamber door, looking devastatingly handsome in a white tunic and a forest-green, belted, plaid kilt; she could see a glimpse of his muscled torso beneath his tunic. The desire that seized her at the sight of him once again took her by surprise, and she swallowed hard.

"I thought ye'd like tae walk with me around the castle grounds."

She stared at him in surprise. Artair had never taken the initiative and requested to walk with her without her father urging him to. When they did take walks, they didn't speak of anything substantial—just the weather, the meals the castle cooks prepared, the good health of her parents.

Now he was looking at her with genuine interest—and hopeful anticipation.

"Ah, yes, my laird—Artair," she corrected herself.

He smiled, and her breath caught in her throat. His smile made him even more handsome. Warmth seared her flesh as he reached out to entwine her arm with his, leading her down the corridor and the winding stairs.

As they made their way out of the castle, she noticed the servants taking them in, some whispering behind their hands. Her mother was right; it seemed as if everyone had noticed the change between them.

"I look forward tae spending more time with ye. I feel I've been remiss in asking more about ye," he said, his blue eyes probing hers, once they stepped out into the courtyard.

"Ye've been very kind," Caitria said hastily. "There's no need tae—"

"I disagree. A husband should ken all there is tae ken about his bride. So tell me something I doonae ken about ye."

The air was brisk, and Artair pulled her in close to his side, his body warming hers. Awareness rippled through her; she trained her gaze resolutely ahead, hoping he didn't notice how much his closeness affected her.

"Ye can tell me," he pressed, at her silence.

"I—I wish tae travel," she said, her voice halting and low, as they made their way past the gates and toward the grounds that surrounded the castle. "And . . . not just tae nearby villages, or even cities. I want tae see what the rest of the world looks like. No one in the castle has gone beyond England, even the nobles. There was a wine merchant who visited the castle once, he'd gone as far as the Mediterranean and he told me—" She stopped herself, embarrassed at her sudden outpour of words, her face flaming. "I'm sorry. Mother tells me 'tis not proper tae discuss such things."

Artair scowled, and her embarrassment deepened. She should have told him she looked forward to having bairns and maintaining his household— something other noble wives looked forward to.

He stopped walking and reached for her hand,

and even more jolts of awareness prickled her skin at his touch.

"There's nothing wrong with discussing yer hopes and dreams with yer future husband. There's nothing wrong with wanting tae travel. Perhaps—perhaps I can take ye tae some of these distant lands."

She blinked with astonishment, hope swelling in her heart. As far as she knew, Artair was perfectly content to live out his days on his land in the north before he took his place as laird of MacGreghor Castle. Not once had he showed any interest in travel—but then again, she'd never discussed her desire to travel with him.

"I—I'd like that," she said, unable to stop the delighted grin that spread across her face. He looked pleased, linking her arm with his as they continued to walk.

"Tell me," he said. "Where would ye like tae go first?"

"Paris," she said immediately. "I'd like tae see the great Cathedral of Notre Dame. And then . . . the walled city of Obidos in Portugal—and York in England."

"Sounds like fine places tae travel," he said, though she now saw conflict in his eyes, and unease simmered within her.

"Is—is there something bothering ye, Artair?" she asked.

He stopped, turning to face her, keeping her

hand clasped in his, his eyes urgent as they probed hers.

"As yer betrothed, 'tis my duty tae protect ye. I must ask—has anything happened as of late . . . anything that would cause ye concern for yer safety?"

For a brief moment, Ferghas's face, his fury raw, his hold on her arm bruising, flashed before her eyes, but she pushed the image away. Ferghas was a beloved member of the clan; he would never harm her.

"No," she said, forcing a smile. "My father keeps me well protected. I've always felt safe here."

He studied her for a long moment as if trying to ascertain the truth of her words. He reached down to touch the side of her face.

"I just want tae keep ye safe, Caitria," he whispered.

Caitria stilled, the awareness that filled her at his touch expanding into the warm rush of desire. His blue eyes fell to her lips, and a hushed, fraught moment stretched between them before he leaned down, seizing her lips with his.

Her heart thudded wildly against her chest as his mouth melded with hers. Her mouth opened, almost of its own volition, and he moaned as his tongue explored her mouth.

He pulled her even closer, and she could feel every inch of his tall, muscular body pressed against hers as his kiss deepened. Her hands reached up, tangling in his hair, hungrily returning his kiss, giving in to the tsunami of pleasure that washed over her. Her entire world was consumed by him, the feel of his strong body against hers, the sweet taste of his kiss.

When he released her, it took several moments to catch her breath. Other than a chaste kiss on the cheek or the forehead, he'd never truly kissed her before.

His eyes met hers, filled with a tumult of both desire—and conflict.

"Caitria—" he began, but stopped himself.

Instead, he took her hand and escorted her all the way back to her chamber without a word, leaving her reeling—and disconcerted—from the fiery passion of his kiss.

CHAPTER 6

*N*iall made his way back to his chamber, cursing himself for kissing Caitria. But he couldn't have stopped himself—the attraction that pulled him toward her was a powerful magnet.

Focus, Niall, he scolded himself. His intention in walking with her had been to see if he could parcel out what—if any—potential danger she might be in. He'd have to force himself to put his scorching desire for her on the back burner. He needed to be friendly toward her—friendly and nothing more—until he could get to the root of what he'd come here for.

He entered his chamber, closing the door behind him and leaning heavily against it.

After Caitria left the feast last night, panic had filled him when he'd realized he was on his own. He'd said as little as possible to the guests who'd approached his table to congratulate him, trying to learn as much as he could about Artair. He'd only been able to discern that Artair was a distant relation to a clan in the north; he had his own manor there, and he was set to marry Caitria in six weeks' time. Before he'd left the feast, Drostan, Caitria's father, had told him he'd imbibed too much ale, and their conversation would have to wait, much to Niall's relief.

The man who'd first approached him on the castle grounds was Latharn, a personal servant of Artair's. Niall had learned from him that the real Artair had been in his chamber before the feast—hence Latharn's surprise at finding "Artair" on the outskirts of the castle grounds. This could only mean that the real Artair had disappeared—to where, he didn't know.

Latharn had seemed mildly suspicious of Niall, cocking his head to the side and studying him for a long moment after leading him to his chamber.

"There's something different about ye," he'd said.

"Just tired from the journey," Niall had said hastily, avoiding the man's eyes.

"Ye told me ye had plenty of rest earlier," Latharn had replied with a frown.

"The fatigue just settled in on me out of nowhere," Niall had returned, and though Latharn had looked at him with a lingering suspicion, he'd nodded and left him alone.

Niall had searched through Artair's belongings to see if there was more he could learn about the man he was impersonating, but there was nothing of note—just a few items of clothing and a fine sword that could only belong to a nobleman.

He'd sat down on the bed, wondering where the actual Artair had disappeared to. Was he somewhere in this time, on the verge of returning to the castle and outing Niall as an imposter? Had they switched places, and Artair was now in the twenty-first century, having taken his place as well?

He'd again tried to recall any such mention of a relative named Artair Dalaigh who bore a striking resemblance to him, but came up empty. Artair Dalaigh must have been someone who barely made a blip on the family radar.

His father had never recounted any similar "switching places" scenarios; he was at a loss over what to do. He'd finally determined that if the real Artair showed up, he would just have to hightail it out of there and get back to Tairseach. In the meantime, he could try to figure out if Caitria was truly in danger—and how to protect her—before returning to his own time. And that didn't include kissing her—or anything of the sort—no matter how lovely she was.

A knock on his door pulled him from his tumble of thoughts. He opened it to find Latharn standing there with a polite smile.

"Laird MacGreghor wishes tae see ye," Latharn said.

Niall nodded his thanks, though unease swirled through his veins. What if Caitria's father had somehow gleaned he was an imposter?

"I heard ye went for a walk with my daughter," Drostan said, by way of greeting, when Niall entered his study moments later. Drostan's brown eyes were jovial, with no hint of suspicion, and Niall relaxed.

"Aye," Niall said, taking the cup of ale Drostan offered him. "I thought we should spend more time together before we're wed."

"I'm glad for it," Drostan said. "I often have tae convince ye tae spend time with my daughter. Though I have tae be honest—I chose ye because ye didnae pursue her the way other suitors did. I doubted ye even desired her—until last night."

Niall only offered him a smile. If Artair didn't desire Caitria, by far the most beautiful woman he'd ever laid eyes on, he was a fool.

Drostan made his way over to the window, looking out, and Niall's gaze fell onto a records' book that lay open on his desk. Niall subtly let his gaze scan the open pages, searching for a year.

And he spotted it, in the top corner, written in Latin. 1390. His estimation had been correct. His historian's mind crawled through several facts about this time period. The Stewarts were in the early days of their centuries-long rule over Scotland, with Robert the Third currently sitting on the Scottish throne. He'd thankfully missed the Black Plague—it hit Scotland several decades before, and the next outbreak wouldn't come until the fifteenth century

But this was still a time of conflict in Scotland—

between the clans and between Scotland and England.

"I love my daughter," Drostan was saying, and Niall detected an undercurrent of powerful emotion in the older man's voice. "More than life itself. Ye ken about my other son . . . the one who died."

"Aye," Niall made himself say, filing away this factoid to memory. When Drostan turned to face him, his eyes glistened with unshed tears.

"I think about him every day. Losing a child is like losing a limb. My Caitria . . . I ken I hold a tight rein on her, but I cannae lose my daughter. And given who I am . . ." He trailed off, a troubled look darting across his expression.

Niall studied him. A picture was now forming. He thought of Caitria, the clear unhappiness in her eyes at the betrothal feast, the longing in her voice when she discussed her desire to travel. Her parents' overprotectiveness was more than just a product of the time—they were overcompensating for the son they'd lost. No wonder Caitria had seemed so uneasy about even discussing travel. It also explained Caitria's age—twenty-five or twenty-six—he guessed. Noblewomen of this time were often married off younger. Her parents must have wanted to keep her here as long as possible before marrying her off. And a man like Drostan MacGreghor had no choice but to marry off his only daughter, given the size of the castle and the lands he must own.

A sudden fear prickled at his chest. What if her parents were onto something? His dreams did point to some danger she was in.

"I'll protect her."

Niall may have been uncertain about what role he played in this time, but he was utterly certain about this. Caitria would come to no harm while he was here. He recalled the hesitation in her eyes when he asked her if she was concerned for her safety. She was hiding something. There was something—or someone—that made her feel unsafe. He'd have to figure out who it was.

The melancholy in Drostan's eyes vanished, and he stepped forward to clap Niall on the shoulder.

"I've chosen well. I'll be proud tae call ye son."

Again, guilt prickled at him; there was genuine affection in Drostan's eyes. He was grateful for the interruption when a servant poked his head inside the room to announce that Drostan had a visitor.

Niall started to leave, but Drostan gestured for him to stay, and Niall turned as a tall man with dark hair and eyes entered. The man's eyes strayed to him, and Niall almost flinched from the malice in his eyes, even as he gave him a polite smile.

"Laird Dalaigh. Laird MacGreghor," the man said, giving Niall and Drostan respectful nods. "I thought I'd invite ye both on tomorrow's hunt with myself and some of the other clan nobles."

"Ah, 'tis kind of ye tae ask, Ferghas," Drostan said. "But I have other matters tae tend tae all day tomorrow. But ye should go, Artair. Ye're a fine hunter and the hunting party will benefit from yer presence."

A fine hunter? Niall's father had taken him on several hunting trips when he was younger, yet he was terrible at it. Dread coursed through his veins. What if Artair was good at everything he was terrible at?

But he just nodded his agreement. *Improvise.*

When a servant entered to call Drostan away, Niall started to trail after him as well, but Ferghas's voice stopped him.

"That was quite the display ye and Caitria put on at the betrothal feast."

Niall turned to face Ferghas. Now that Drostan had left the study, the malice in Ferghas's eyes was plain, his lips curled back in a sneer.

"Ye've never looked at her the way ye did last night. I wonder what's changed," Ferghas continued, taking a threatening step forward.

Niall stiffened. It would do him no good to make enemies in this time, but he couldn't stymie a wave of hot anger that swept over him at Ferghas's words.

"I believe what occurs between me and my betrothed is none of yer concern," he bit out.

Ferghas's eyes darkened as he took another menacing step forward. Though Ferghas was tall, Niall was taller, and he straightened to his full height.

"I care for Caitria a great deal. If it wasnae for

ye, I'd be the one wedding her. I doonae ken what ye're up tae . . . but there's something different about ye. And if ye mean my Caitria harm—"

"She's not yer Caitria," Niall snapped, startled by the sudden anger that seized him. "And I repeat —the relationship between me and my betrothed is none of yer concern."

"And I'll have tae remind ye," Ferghas coldly returned, "I'm one of the most respected members of this clan. Her father trusts me above all—even ye. Ye havenae married the lass yet. Ye're still an outsider."

"An outsider who's wedding the laird's daughter," Niall said, taking pleasure in the angry flush that spread across Ferghas's face.

A charged silence stretched, the threat of violence thick in the air. But Ferghas moved past him to the door, his jaw clenched.

"I'll see ye on tomorrow's hunt."

The threat in his tone was undeniable.

His encounter with Ferghas filled him with an unease that lingered for the rest of the day, even as he tried to learn as much as he could about Artair from Latharn without being too obvious. All he could glean from Latharn was that Artair kept to himself, he didn't have a lot of close friends and seemed content to keep it that way, but he got along well with Drostan and the other clan nobles.

When Niall sat down next to Caitria for supper in the great hall, his unease dissipated at the sight of her. He didn't know if it was because she was his anchor, the person who had inadvertently drawn him to his time—or if it was just her presence alone. He suspected it was both.

Her eyes met his as he sat, and a lovely flush spread over her face; he suspected she was recalling their kiss.

"Tell me more of these lands ye wish tae visit," he murmured, wanting to put her at ease, after a servant placed a meal of herring and carrots before them.

"I—I'm content tae live in yer castle, Artair," she said, lowering her gaze to her plate. "I ken what my duty is."

He studied the dullness in her eyes, wondering what had changed the vibrant woman of earlier into this dutiful robot once more. His eyes strayed across the hall to her parents, who watched them with open approval. They seemed kind, and he could tell they loved Caitria deeply, yet they seemed to be the key to her unhappiness.

He knew he should make no promises for a future he wouldn't share with her, but he wanted to put the light back into her eyes.

"When ye're in my household . . . it will be yer needs that I tend tae, not yer parents."

He didn't realize the potential double meaning of his words until Caitria's face flamed hot, her eyes flying to his in scandalized surprise.

But that didn't stop the teasing smile that curved his lips.

After a stunned beat, she returned his smile.

"What is it that ye want tae do?" he asked suddenly, giving her a wink. "Right now?"

"Right now?" she echoed.

"Right now," he repeated, firm.

"Well, there's a loch not far from the castle grounds. My brother Tadhg and I used tae play on its shores," she said, with a wistful look in her eyes.

He got to his feet with a grin.

"Let us take our leave," he said, extending his hand.

CHAPTER 7

*C*aitria wrapped her arms around Artair's waist, warmth spiraling through her at the feel of his body against hers. They had gone to the stables after leaving the hall, ignoring the startled looks of the other guests. They'd awakened a stable boy from his nap to fetch her favorite horse, Kerr.

Caitria had directed Artair toward the loch. She leaned into Artair as they rode, reveling in not just the feel of him, but the sensation of the night breeze whipping through her hair, and the faint scent of moisture in the air that hinted of coming rain. She often forgot how stifled she felt when confined to the castle, and she intended to revel in these brief moments of freedom.

Artair slowed Kerr down to a trot as they arrived at Loch Romond. He dismounted and tied Kerr to a nearby tree before helping Caitria down. Tendrils of pleasure fissured through her at his touch, and she had to turn away from his disconcerting draw to walk toward the loch, taking in the beauty of its shimmering waters beneath the moonlight.

"I loved coming here when I was just a girl. Our parents didnae want us tae swim here, but Tadhg and I convinced our maid tae let us," she said, smiling at the memory. Yet a sudden sharp pang of grief splintered her heart, and she blinked back tears.

She never let herself dwell too much on thoughts of her late brother, because whenever she did, an overwhelming grief consumed her. Her brother had been the kindest man she knew and possessed the same joviality of their father. He'd encouraged her to step out of the shelter their parents created and explore the world as she wished.

"When I'm chief of the clan, ye'll be able tae follow yer heart's desire," he'd told her, in all sincerity.

His sudden death during a hunting accident had shocked and aggrieved their entire clan. Caitria still thought of him every day: the sound of his laughter, the glint in his green eyes whenever they shared a jest.

Artair was silent, and when she looked up at him, the look he gave her was filled with patience; he was telling her without words to continue. Caitria was the one who usually listened; none of her suitors had ever let her get a word in as they prattled on.

"Sometimes . . . I wonder what he'd be doing now," she continued. "He would be the heir, and my father would be rid of me."

"I doonae think he wants tae be rid of ye," Artair said gently. "Yer father loves ye. Ye're fortunate tae have that."

A wistful look flickered across his expression, and she wondered if he was thinking of his own father. Drostan had told her Artair's father died long ago. She waited, hoping he would say more, but he remained silent, his eyes trained on the glittering waters of the loch.

Impulsively, she lifted the hem of her gown, slipping off her shoes to move to the edge of the shore, allowing the waters to lap against her bare feet.

"What do ye do on a daily basis?" Artair asked. "It seems like ye rarely get tae do what ye enjoy."

Artair removed his shoes, moving to stand on the edge of the shore next to her.

"It doesnae matter what I enjoy," she said, stiffening. "I'm the sole heir and I have my duties. I'm tae marry ye and run yer household."

But Artair's perceptive gaze was unrelenting.

"I ken ye want tae travel. What else? When's the last time ye did something for yerself?" he pressed.

Caitria searched her mind. She couldn't remember. For the past several years she'd spent her days being groomed to become a wife and the lady of a castle.

"This," she said, and Artair's expression softened with sympathy. He stepped closer to her, and heat darted along her skin.

"Life doesnae always have tae be about duty," he said.

"What about ye?" she challenged, irritation rippling through her. She didn't want his pity. "I ken ye're marrying me out of a sense of duty."

"Aye," he said, and though she'd known this to be true, a sharp pang of disappointment pierced her at his blunt acknowledgment. "But I also make room in my life for the things that I enjoy."

"And what do ye enjoy?" she asked, partially as a challenge, partially out of genuine curiosity—there was much she didn't know about him.

He hesitated, his expression shuttering.

"I—ride," he said finally. "And I read. I read a great deal when I doonae have matters of my lands and manor tae tend tae."

He wasn't looking at her, and she suspected his words weren't altogether truthful.

"What else?" she asked.

"What else?" he echoed, with a puzzled frown.

"I've told ye my dreams of traveling—what of ye? What do ye dream of?"

For a moment, he looked stricken, before his expression went carefully blank.

"Well?" she pressed.

"I'm—sure ye ken already," he muttered.

"Are ye making a jest?" she asked with a laugh of disbelief. "Ye've barely spoken a word tae me the few times we've met in private, other than tae discuss something general like the coming rains or the health of my family. 'Tis only recently that ye've taken an interest in me. There's something different about ye, Artair. What's changed?"

He paled, and Caitria's heart picked up its pace—there *was* a reason for the change in him.

When he spoke, his eyes were still guarded, his words careful.

"I've never thought about my hopes and dreams. I suppose I've also spent my life focusing on duty. I've just . . . followed in my father's footsteps."

She stepped closer, studying him intently. Though he'd evaded her question, she only saw truth in his eyes.

"I suppose that's what we have in common," she said, turning back to face the glittering waters of the loch. "I love my parents . . . 'tis why I do what they ask of me, as stifled as I feel sometimes."

"Aye," Artair said, his smile a little sad. "I can understand that. As I said . . . I do envy ye of yer father's love. I never saw my own father much."

Empathy filled her at the look of pained longing on his face, and she reached for his hand.

"Well . . . 'tis good ye're marrying his daughter. Ye'll be his son by marriage."

Artair's smile faded, and he looked guarded once more—and torn.

"Artair, what is it?" she asked. "Is there something ye're not telling me?"

He hesitated, reaching out to cup her face. She became increasingly aware of their proximity, and her heart thundered in her chest.

"I—I just want tae keep ye safe," he whispered, his voice wavering.

She met his eyes, no longer caring that he'd again evaded her question. She recalled the feel of his lips on hers, and ached for him to kiss her again . . .

He granted her her wish. With a strangled groan he pulled her close, his lips plundering hers. He thoroughly explored her mouth with his, and she met his kiss eagerly, his lips soft yet demanding against hers. His masculine scent infused her nostrils, and she whimpered as she clung to him, her need for him growing as their kiss deepened.

When he released her, his eyes were a storm of conflict and desire—just as they'd been after their first kiss.

"Let's get ye back tae the castle," he said gruffly. "We'll not want yer father tae worry."

Caitria dreamed of Artair that night. The feel of his body against hers, the taste of him, the desire that seared every part of her like fire at his touch. She'd assumed she would have a polite relationship with her husband, dutifully bedding him when it was time to make an heir . . . but now, she knew it would be much more than that. For the first time, she longed for a man's touch . . . the touch of her husband-to-be.

But when she awoke, she recalled his distance, the conflict in his eyes after they kissed. She was to be his bride . . . what was the reason for it? He'd evaded her questions about the changes in him, and she was surprised by how much she wanted him to share himself with her. She'd shared a part of herself with him by confessing her dreams of travel . . . why couldn't he do the same?

"What has yer thoughts entangled so?" her mother asked the next morning, as they sat in Liusaidh's private chamber, working on their embroidery.

Caitria swallowed, focusing on poking her needle through the plaid fabric. She'd thought it would irritate her parents that she and Artair had fled during the feast, but instead they'd been pleased.

She bit her lip, lowering her embroidery and studying her mother. Given that her parents had such favor for her and Artair's relationship, perhaps she could give her advice.

"He's gotten me tae open up tae him . . . but I cannae get him tae do the same. Was it like this for ye and Father?"

"Aye," Liusaidh said, smiling at the memory. "But I was the shy, closed off one, yer father the open one."

"How did he get ye tae open up?"

"I fell in love with him," Liusaidh said simply,

and defeat settled in over her. While Artair now desired her, she knew it was far from love.

"Caitria, my darling bairn," Liusaidh said with a sigh, setting down her embroidery and reaching out to take her hand. "Artair cares for ye; I can tell by the way he looks at ye. I think love will soon follow."

Caitria gave her a jerky nod, though she didn't think this was true.

Her mother studied her, and Caitria knew she wanted to push the matter further, but Caitria didn't want to discuss it anymore.

"Have the seamstresses finished with my potential dresses for the wedding?" she asked, as a purposeful diversion.

It was the right thing to say, as her mother eagerly launched into discussing the seamstress's progress, while a wave of conflicting emotions swept over Caitria at the thought of wedding Artair: uncertainty, desire . . . and hope.

If it weren't for Ferghas's cold eyes on Niall, studying his every move, he would have enjoyed going on a fourteenth-century hunt. It was fascinating to see what modern historians had gotten right—and what they'd gotten wrong about such hunts.

Their party consisted of a couple dozen men, including himself and Latharn—some on horse, some on foot—stalking silently through the forest with their weapons at the ready, searching for the wild boars that roamed the forest. It wasn't too different from modern-day hunts; the only glaring difference was the lack of guns.

But he was unable to concentrate on the intricacies of the hunt. Memories of Caitria's lovely body pressed against his and the sweetness of her kiss filled his thoughts.

And there was the matter of Ferghas. While the other nobles treated him with polite friendliness, Ferghas was brusque and kept asking him probing questions.

At the start of the hunt, when Niall failed to slay a deer with his arrow, Ferghas's eyes narrowed.

"I thought ye were a good hunter," he said, his voice loud enough to carry to the other nobles. "Chieftain MacGreghor has sung yer praises."

Niall's mouth went tight. He kept hearing of Artair's hunting prowess, so he tried to avoid killing any boars and focused on engaging in light conversation with the other nobles, making sure to only discuss easy topics such as the fair weather or the demeanor of the beasts who stalked this forest.

He was relieved that he could at least ride a horse; it was something his father had taught him, insisting that every good historian should be able to master the most common method of transport of the past.

"I'm just distracted with thoughts of my bride-tae-be," he said, meeting Ferghas's gaze with silent challenge. The other nobles chuckled and gave him good-natured grins, while Ferghas's expression darkened.

"The chief wouldnae like ye speaking of his daughter in such a manner," Ferghas growled, as the rest of their party ventured ahead.

"Chief MacGreghor is quite happy at the closeness between me and my bride-tae-be. He kens I mean no disrespect," Niall returned. He thought of the feel of Caitria's body against his, and a surge of possessiveness flowed through him. "I've just learned tae appreciate what's mine."

What are you doing, Niall? he scolded himself. After his previous encounter with Ferghas, he'd told himself that he would stay out of the man's way—he couldn't afford to make enemies in this time. But he didn't appreciate the man's obvious jealousy, and there was something about Ferghas that made him uneasy . . . something that made Niall wonder if he was the source of danger toward Caitria. A jealous man could be a dangerous man.

A celebratory whoop from one of the nobles interrupted their tense face-off, and Niall clenched his jaw, stepping away from Ferghas to approach a friendly noble by the name of Muir, congratulating him on his successful kill.

He forced his focus away from Ferghas, trying to learn what he could from the other nobles without being too obvious. It was a close-knit group, with the nobles sharing inside jokes and good-natured laughter among themselves. Their camaraderie was easy to join, and he had to actively suppress his guilt over his deception, reminding himself that he was doing this for Caitria's sake.

They all seemed to like Artair, and none of them seemed suspicious of him, though a couple of men joked that he was less taciturn than usual. It was only Ferghas who trained dark, suspicious eyes on him.

Niall ignored Ferghas as their party fell silent;

they'd approached a large clearing, where several boars roamed.

The men spread out. Niall, remembering that Artair was a seasoned hunter, followed suit, trailed by Latharn, until they were alone on the edge of the clearing.

The sudden buzz of an arrow careening through the air toward him made Niall whirl in surprise.

"My laird!" Latharn shouted, shoving him out of the way, and Niall stumbled back in astonishment as an arrow narrowly missed him, burrowing itself in the flesh of Latharn's shoulder instead.

Niall raced to Latharn's side, kneeling down as Latharn sank to the ground, crying out in pain as he clutched his shoulder. Panicked, Niall tore away the fabric of his tunic. His shoulder was bleeding, but luckily it looked like the arrow had just grazed his flesh.

He looked up to find Ferghas standing a few yards away, his eyes venomous as he lowered his bow and arrow. A chill coursed through Niall; this was no accident.

"Latharn!" Ferghas said, schooling his features into a look of concern as he approached. "I cannae believe I did that—I was aiming for one of the boars. Are ye all right?"

"He's just been shot by yer arrow," Niall snapped, tearing off a strip of fabric from his tunic and wrapping it around Latharn's shoulder. "He's not all right."

"'Tis just a flesh wound," Latharn said, though his face was pale with pain.

"Let's get ye back tae the castle healer," Ferghas said, moving forward to help haul him up along with Niall, as the other nobles gathered around with looks of growing concern.

As they led Latharn out of the forest, Niall met Ferghas's eyes. Ferghas's eyes met his, filled with malevolence, and he knew without a shadow of a doubt that Ferghas had been aiming for him, and he doubted he'd just wanted to graze his shoulder. He'd indeed made an enemy in the fourteenth-century—and had likely found the person who was a danger to Caitria.

~

"What is this, my laird?" Latharn asked with a frown.

"A . . . concoction I picked up while traveling," Niall said, handing him one of the pills of penicillin he'd brought with him. "It'll help yer wound heal faster."

He'd come to Latharn's small chamber after the castle healer had tended to him, intent on giving him the penicillin he'd brought. Though the healer had done a good job tending to Latharn's wound, Niall knew how common—and dangerous—infections were in this time.

Latharn hesitated, eyeing the tablet suspiciously for a long moment. Pills wouldn't be invented until the nineteenth century, so he knew it must look odd to Latharn.

"I got it from a doctor in Edinburgh; he's treated many a wound like yers," Niall lied, giving him an encouraging smile.

Latharn still looked reluctant, but took it, and Niall had to direct him how to swallow it down.

"When did ye go tae Edinburgh? Ye've not left these lands in some time," Latharn asked, after he'd swallowed the pill.

Niall hesitated. He needed to be careful with what he said; it was too easy to contradict the movements of the true Artair.

"It was some time ago," he said dismissively. "I cannae thank ye enough, Latharn," he continued, with genuine sincerity. Latharn had saved his life.

"'Twas nothing ye wouldnae have done for me, my laird," Latharn said, with a look of intense loyalty. Niall studied him, wondering what Artair had done to inspire such loyalty. "And 'twas an accident. Ferghas visited me, he was most aggrieved by what happened."

Niall stiffened at the mention of Ferghas. He wanted to ask him more about Ferghas, to find out everything he could about him, but he didn't know how much the real Artair knew about him.

"Ye rest now," he said finally, giving Latharn a nod before leaving.

"Artair."

Niall halted as Caitria approached Latharn's chamber, her green eyes wide with worry. She rushed to him, and surprise—then warmth—flowed through him as she threw her arms around his neck.

"I heard there was an accident," she said, suddenly looking shy as she released him. "I—I was worried."

His heart swelled at the realization that her worry was for him, and then a heaviness settled over him as he recalled that her brother had died during a hunting accident.

"I'm fine," he murmured, reaching out to give her hands a reassuring squeeze. He looked around the corridor; servants bustled to and fro. He needed to talk to her alone.

"I'll escort ye tae yer chamber," he said, keeping her hand in his as he led her back down the corridor.

Once they were alone in her chamber, he turned to face her.

"I need tae ask ye something."

"Aye?"

"'Tis about Ferghas," he said, and there was no mistaking her flinch as she met his eyes. "How long have ye been acquainted with him?"

She stiffened, removing her hands from his and lowering her gaze.

"He's been a friend of the family's—and my father's—for years. Everyone in the clan adores him."

He studied her closely. She held herself rigid and avoided his gaze.

A sudden and fierce wave of protectiveness

swept over him. Had Ferghas harmed her? Threatened her?

"Has Ferghas . . . done anything tae ye?" he growled. "Harmed ye in any way?"

"No," she said quickly, too quickly. "Why—why are ye asking me about Ferghas?"

Because he's dangerous, he wanted to say. *Because I think he may be linked to the danger you're in.*

"I doonae trust him," he said instead. He decided to not mention the hunting incident—for now. He didn't want to bring back painful memories of her brother's death. "I want ye tae stay away from him."

He braced himself for questions or protests, but she nodded her head in quick agreement—which proved she was already wary of Ferghas.

"Of course," she said, her tone taking on that formality once more. "As a betrothed woman, it would be improper for me tae visit with another man alone."

He regarded her warily. There was that polite facade again.

"Ye can confide in me," he said, ignoring the splinter of guilt in his chest, as he added, "we're tae be wed."

Something shifted in her eyes—joy? wariness? —before it vanished, and she gave him a stiff nod.

"Is there anything else I can do for ye, m'laird?"

Both annoyance and desire propelled him forward. He wrapped his arms around her, tugging her into the circle of his arms. Her lovely eyes widened in astonishment, her lips parting, and lusty images of the things he could do with that mouth filled his mind.

"I told ye," he said. "Call me—" He wanted to tell her his true name, but he forced out the false one anyway. "—Artair."

"Artair," she whispered. His desire spiked, and he couldn't help himself; he needed another taste of her . . .

He sealed his lips to hers in a kiss. She moaned against him, and he pulled her closer, reveling in the feel of her taut nipples brushing against his chest through his tunic. How easy it would be to lift her up into his arms, to carry her to the bed, to taste every sweet inch of her before claiming her body with his own. He'd never wanted another woman as much as he wanted her; just the feel of her body against his was sweet torture.

But he forced himself to release her and stepped back. She looked up at him, wide-eyed and breathless.

"Remember what I said," he murmured, his voice husky with restrained desire. "Ye can confide in me. And never call me 'my laird' again . . . or I'll be tempted tae remind ye just who I am tae ye."

CHAPTER 9

*L*ong after Artair left her chamber, his kiss still lingered on Caitria's lips. She didn't see him again until supper in the great hall, yet she could hardly concentrate on her meal; her gaze kept straying to his mouth in spite of herself. His blue eyes met hers, and she swallowed hard, discerning the desire that lurked in their depths.

She hoped he would walk with her after supper, or at least escort her to her chamber. Instead, he gave her a polite nod and left with her father when supper came to an end, and disappointment twisted her gut.

As she tried to drift off to sleep that night, intrusive thoughts of making love circled through her mind. And not in the cursory way she'd thought of it before—wondering how much pain there would be during her first time, or how often she would have to do it. Instead, she found herself imagining it . . . in detail. Would Artair take his time with her? Would he put his lips on every part of her skin, teasing her before finally claiming her body with his own? Would his blue eyes darken with desire, the way they did when he kissed her, with his name on her lips when their bodies joined?

She turned onto her side, recalling the gossip she'd overheard from her maids about the act of lovemaking.

"My husband doesnae take his time," one maid had complained to another. "He's done only moments after entering me."

"Men look ridiculous when they reach their release and spill their seed," she'd overheard another maid whisper with a giggle. "'Tis difficult tae not laugh when my Daklen has his release."

She didn't think Artair would look ridiculous when he reached his release. She pictured his handsome features strained with desire, his breathy moan as he spilled his seed inside her . . .

Caitria awoke with a gasp. She'd fallen asleep with those scandalously erotic thoughts about Artair.

Ailsa entered her chamber and Caitria lowered her gaze, as if to hide the erotic thoughts that had dominated her mind.

"'Tis time tae wake, my lady," Ailsa said, placing a gown on her bed. "The laird wants tae see ye."

"The laird?" she asked, unable to keep the eagerness out of her tone. Artair wanted to see her?

"Yer father," Ailsa amended, her lips twitching in amusement at the obvious disappointment in Caitria's eyes.

Setting aside her disappointment, Caitria dressed and went to find her father, who waited for her in the courtyard. He beamed, his brown eyes lighting up at the sight of her.

"Good morning tae ye," he said, linking arms with her and leading her out of the courtyard.

"Good morning," she returned with a polite smile. "Is . . . there a reason ye wanted tae see me?"

"Cannae I just wish tae see my daughter? I've not seen ye alone for some time," he said.

He was right. Before her betrothal, Drostan would often send for her just to walk with him around the grounds of the castle and inquire about her day, listening intently to her responses. Unlike other noblewomen of the clan, whose fathers barely spent time with them, her father went out of his way to spend time with her—especially after Tadhg's death.

"Yer mother and I are pleased that ye and Artair are getting along so well," he was saying now. "The day of yer wedding draws near. Everyone of importance in the clan will be in attendance."

Only days ago, dread would have tightened her chest at the thought of her upcoming wedding. But as she recalled Artair's words, of taking her to the distant lands she dreamed of, excitement darted through her.

"I cannae believe it. My only daughter soon tae

be wed," Drostan said with a sad sigh. "When ye were still a bairn, I'd watch ye and Tadhg playing in the courtyard, and I'd think—those two are the loves of my life. Ye and my Liusaidh."

Caitria stopped, moved by the emotion in her father's voice.

"I'll come visit ye often. Ye have my word."

"I shall hope so," he said with a wink. "If that husband of yers will let ye out of his sight."

Caitria smiled, a spark of delight dancing through her at his description of Artair as her husband.

They continued to walk in companionable silence, and when they returned to the castle, Artair was heading out the front doors; Drostan passed her off to him with a pleased smile.

Caitria wondered if desire could make a man even more handsome and drank in the sight of him. His white tunic was partially opened to reveal his muscular chest beneath, and he wore a plaid tartan kilt of deep crimson, his sword sheathed at his side.

He gave her a heart-stopping smile before taking her hand without a word and leading her away from the castle.

"Where are we going?" she asked with a startled laugh.

"'Tis a surprise," he said with a wink, leading her toward the stables. "The stable boy tells me ye have a favorite horse?"

"Aye. Her name is Kerr," Caitria said, pleasantly surprised that Artair had cared enough to ask.

She led him to Kerr, who was tied up in the rear of the stables.

He helped her onto the horse before climbing on behind her, and they tore out of the stables.

They rode past the familiar moors that surrounded the castle, and excitement swirled through her as they kept riding past the familiar lands.

They didn't stop until they reached a waterfall, tucked deep within a thick patch of forest, nestled between two jagged hills comprised of craggy rocks. The rushing waters of the waterfall spilled into a small, meandering stream. Sunlight shafted through the trickling waters and lit up its deep blue waters.

Caitria shook her head in awe. She'd never known such a sight existed so close to the castle.

"How have I never seen this before?" she whispered.

"Because ye've rarely ventured beyond the castle grounds," he said, coming to stand at her side. "It may not be far from yer castle . . . but there are ways to travel without going very far."

"Thank ye for showing this tae me," she said, beaming. But she went rigid at the thought of her parents. It'd worry them if they knew she'd left the castle grounds. "But my parents—"

"For once, doonae concern yerself with what yer parents will think. Only think about ye for now," he said gently.

She obliged, pushing thoughts of her parents to

the back of her mind. She slipped off her shoes and moved to the edge of the stream, getting as close to the waterfall as she could, closing her eyes to savor the sound of the rushing water over the rocks.

She felt Artair's presence close behind her and turned. It seemed like the most natural thing in the world when his head dipped and his lips met hers. They kissed hungrily, Caitria clinging to him as he thoroughly explored her mouth. Caitria savored every moment of their kiss—his hands holding her body close, the slight scrape of his stubble beneath her fingers as she lifted her hands up to his face, the soft insistence of his lips probing hers.

He released her with great reluctance, but kept her in his arms, pressing her back against his torso as they turned back to face the waterfall.

"My father took me tae a waterfall like this, once," he said. "'Tis one of the few times I can remember him spending a prolonged time with me."

She turned to face him, delighted that he was telling her something personal.

"'Tis odd . . . I was still a boy, and I can only remember fragments of that day. The pressure of his hand on mine as he took me close tae the rushing waters. The sound of his voice—it seemed tae me so very deep when I was a lad—as he explained the history of the place. The delight in his eyes when I asked questions." His blue eyes filled with sadness. "We didnae have many moments like that."

"I'm sorry," she murmured, her heart filling with sympathy. Melancholy filled his eyes, and she wanted to do what she could to chase his sadness away. "Ye still havenae told me what interests ye."

He studied her for a long moment, and she thought he wouldn't answer, until he finally said, "History."

"History?"

"Aye. Things that have happened in the distant past. I enjoy reading about such events . . . studying them, trying tae figure out why they happened."

His eyes brightened as he spoke, no longer filled with the sadness of moments before. She'd never known anyone who concerned themselves with events of the past, especially a Highland laird. Their concerns seemed to only lie with their lands and property, or conflicts with other clans. Artair had never mentioned such an interest before. It again struck her how little she knew the man she was going to marry.

"My tutors taught me about ancient Greece and Rome," she said. "Their great leaders . . . the grand buildings they made, many of which still stand. 'Tis when I first started tae dream of travel, tae long tae see such things for myself."

"'Tis one of my favorite time periods tae read about," he said, his face lighting up, like a torchlight cast onto darkness. "Ye can still see remnants of Emperor Hadrian's wall south of here."

"Maybe ye can take me there one day," she said,

a rush of excitement coursing through her at the thought. "After we're wed."

He stiffened, and it was as if a door had been abruptly shut, the guard in his eyes returning. She removed herself from his arms, frowning.

"Artair?" she asked, and he flinched at the sound of his name. "Artair, what's wrong?"

"Caitria," he whispered, reaching out to touch her face. "There's . . . so much I wish I could tell ye."

"Like what?" she pressed. She took his hand, imploring him with her eyes. "Artair . . . ye can tell me whatever it is. We're tae be wed. We shouldnae have secrets between us."

Her words seemed to only increase his guardedness.

"We should get back," he said, his voice strained. She watched him walk back to Kerr, a shard of hurt pricking her at his sudden coldness.

As they rode back, a heavy dread replaced the joy that had infused her. She was now certain he was hiding something from her, and it surprised her how much this bothered her. She almost wished they were still polite strangers—then she wouldn't care so much. But her physical hunger for him had awakened an emotional hunger, and she was starved for any emotional scraps she could get from him.

When they returned to the castle, he left her at her chamber door with a curt bow. She watched him go, an idea seizing her.

Caitria hurried to her father's study, which was thankfully empty. She searched until she found a leather-bound manuscript on one of his cabinets. She'd have to ask her father's permission to gift the manuscript, but she had no doubt he'd agree. She hoped this gift would help Artair open up to her.

"My lady."

Caitria stilled at the sound of Ferghas's voice behind her as she exited her father's study. She turned to face him, wary, recalling Artair's warning. But his handsome face was warm and kind, and for a moment she hesitated, wondering if she'd overreacted during their last encounter—and if Artair was wrong about him.

"I've been searching for ye," he said.

"I went riding with Artair," she returned, and started to walk away, but he blocked her path. His expression darkened, the jealousy in his expression unmistakable.

"Ye should be careful of him, Caitria."

She gritted her teeth, again moving to step past him.

"He's tae be my husband, I've nothing tae fear from him. Now, if ye will kindly move—"

"There's something different about him," he said. She hesitated, only for a moment, but he caught it. "Ye ken it tae be true."

She stilled, thinking of those tiny, indiscernible differences she'd noticed about Artair, and her growing certainty that he was hiding something from her.

"I care about ye, Caitria," Ferghas said, stepping close to her—too close. He reached out to touch her face, and she acted on pure instinct. She stepped on his foot.

He cursed and stumbled back, looking genuinely shocked. Shock coursed through her as well—she'd never done something so bold before. She stilled as a rage she'd never seen in Ferghas before flashed across his face, and he took a threatening step toward her. He halted when two giggling servants passed by, and his rage melted away, replaced by a bright, affable smile. A chill crept down her arms—it was like watching someone put on a mask.

"Think of what I've said, my lady," he said, giving her a brusque bow before leaving her.

She watched him go, shaken by the rage she'd seen in his eyes—yet his warning lingered.

There's something different about Artair.

CHAPTER 10

*L*ong after he'd returned to the castle, Niall paced his chamber, raking his hand through his hair. He knew that Caitria was disappointed when his guard went up—but it had been on the tip of his tongue to tell her the truth, consequences be damned. Every time she called him Artair, it was hard not to flinch. The small flare of guilt that had initially filled him at his inadvertent deception had grown into a full-fledged flame; he didn't know how much longer he could keep up the pretense—especially now that he cared for and desired her so much.

He had to remind himself, over and over again, that she belonged to the actual Artair, someone who belonged in this time. He needed to focus on the reason he'd come to this time in the first place—to rescue her from the danger that threatened her. And that danger, he was certain, was Ferghas.

Ever since the hunting incident, an unsettling

suspicion had taken root in his mind. Caitria's brother Tadhg had died during a hunting accident. While Ferghas was definitely an arse, was he also a murderer? Had he killed Tadhg, who was the heir, to seize power for himself after marrying Caitria?

By the time Caitria had a servant fetch him to her father's study the next day, his dark suspicion about Ferghas had firmly taken hold. But he was uncertain if he should share his suspicions about him, given that he had no concrete proof.

He found her standing in the center of her father's study, giving him a hesitant smile, and a sense of déjà vu struck him. His chest tightened as he realized that he'd seen this moment before, in one of his dreams. Her standing before him, giving him a shy smile, wearing the same ruby gown she wore now.

Her smile faltered as he stiffened.

"Artair?" she asked. "Is something the matter?"

"No," he forced himself to say, giving her a smile that he hoped was warm. "I'm glad ye sent for me. Why are we in yer father's study?"

"I . . . I have a gift for ye," she said, biting her lip. She turned to the desk, picking up a leather-bound manuscript and handing it to him.

"Ye told me ye liked stories of ancient Rome. Father is friendly with a man who has a manuscript workshop in Edinburgh," she continued. "He sends us books of the hours for prayers and sometimes sends additional books like this. Father allowed me tae gift it tae ye. 'Tis the writings of the Roman historian Suetonius."

Niall looked down at the leather-bound manuscript in awe. It was made of parchment, Suetonius's writings carefully inscribed onto the pages in brown ink. His historian's instinct made him want to grab a pair of gloves to examine it—in modern times, a book like this would be worth a fortune. Most manuscripts made during this time period were religious works and books of prayer, not works of literature—or even works of history.

He swallowed hard as he studied it; as far as he knew, no such copies of this book existed in his own time. Many such books were lost in fires or natural disasters over the centuries.

"Do ye like it?" she asked, her tone uneasy at his prolonged silence.

"This is the most precious gift anyone has ever given to me," he said, in all sincerity. She smiled at his response, her entire face lighting up.

Past girlfriends had given him fancy watches and cufflinks as gifts, and he'd wondered if any of them had known him at all. But this fourteenth-century beauty had known that this would please him, had gone out of her way to gift him with something that would make him happy.

He made his decision right then and there; he was going to tell her the truth, and he'd just have to deal with the consequences. But he needed to do it at the right time—and the right place.

"I've a surprise for ye as well," he said.

"Aye?" she asked, her lovely face brightening with delight. "What is it?"

He leaned forward, unable to resist placing a brief kiss on her lips. "I cannae tell ye, lass. That's why 'tis a surprise. Ye'll find out soon."

The look of pure joy on her face was infectious. He grinned, reaching out to pull her close, their lips meeting in a fervent kiss.

God, he wanted this woman. He didn't care that they were in her father's study. He wanted to spread her out on the desk, hike up her skirts, and taste the sweetness between her thighs before sinking into her depths. Hot arousal coiled through him at the thought, and Caitria let out a startled moan against his mouth as she felt his growing erection against her body.

"Enough of all this," a wary but amused voice said from behind them, and they abruptly broke apart as Drostan entered.

Caitria's face flamed, and a rush of guilt and shame surged through him. He should have shown more restraint.

"Yer wedding day will be here soon enough," Drostan continued.

"I—I'm sorry, Father," Caitria stammered, her face flaming. "I—I should return tae my chamber."

She fled before he could reply, and Drostan watched her go with amusement.

"I'm sorry," Niall said. "I doonae mean any disrespect—"

But Drostan waved away his apology, still looking amused.

"My daughter has been happier since ye arrived. I doonae ken what's changed in the last few weeks between ye two, but I'm glad for it. Just doonae use my study for yer amorous attentions—wait till she's yer wife proper.

"Aye. Of course," Niall said, relieved by Drostan's surprising nonchalance. The chastity of noblewomen was especially prized at this time; he suspected Drostan wouldn't behave so kindly toward him if he knew of the thoughts that had gone through his mind just moments before.

"I'd like tae ask yer permission, while ye're here," Niall said, deciding to take advantage of Drostan's good mood. "I'd like tae take yer daughter tae Inverness for a day or two. Get her out of the castle for a spell before the wedding."

Niall decided that if he was going to tell her the truth, he wanted them to be alone and away from the castle, where there would be no chance of being overheard.

"Ah," Drostan said, his look of amusement vanishing, replaced by a dark frown. "I see my daughter has expressed tae ye her desire tae travel."

Niall silently cursed; he didn't want this to backfire and cause Caitria trouble.

"She hasnae asked me tae take her anywhere. This is all my choice," he said, keeping his tone even. "With yer permission, of course."

Drostan hesitated for a long moment, his mouth tight.

"Very well," he said finally, to Niall's immense relief. "But I want guards tae accompany ye on yer journey.

"Aye," Niall said, smiling. "I thank ye."

"My daughter doesnae ken what dangers lie beyond our lands. As her husband-to-be, I trust ye'll keep her safe, but I'll not have her taking any more journeys beyond my lands after this."

Niall stared at him, trying to keep his expression amenable. For someone who loved his daughter so much, Drostan didn't seem to fathom how much he was suffocating her.

As if reading his thoughts, Drostan gave him a long look.

"Ye'll ken how I feel when ye and Caitria have bairns of yer own," he said, and for a split second, an image of Caitria, plump and swollen with his child, filled his mind. He had to ignore the joy that flared through him at the thought.

That will never happen, he reminded himself, as he left Drostan's study. *Especially once you tell her the truth. She may kick you out of her life for good—and you'll never see her again.*

CHAPTER 11

"Are ye going tae tell me what the surprise is now?" Caitria asked, stepping out into the courtyard.

Niall smiled down at her. It was early the next morning, and Caitria had pestered him for hints about the surprise during supper in the great hall last night, and then when he'd escorted her to her chamber—he'd had to silence her with a thorough kiss.

"I'm taking ye on a trip," he said. "We're going tae Inverness."

Inverness was a relatively small village at this time, but given the look of sheer awe on her face, he might as well have told her they were traveling to the moon.

"Inverness," she breathed. "I've never been."

She grinned, throwing her arms around him. He held her close, closing his eyes. He would tell her the truth about who he really was during their trip, so he was determined to relish her happiness in this moment, before she learned of his deception.

He'd decided that he would give her time to enjoy Inverness before dropping his bombshell. If she sent him away, he could at least tell her his suspicions about Ferghas and pray that would be enough to keep her out of any danger Ferghas posed to her. Tairseach wasn't too far from Inverness; he could make his way back to his own time, knowing he'd done all that he could.

He tried to ignore the ache that spread throughout his gut at the mere thought of leaving her, reminding himself that his plan was always to return to his own time.

He helped her up onto Kerr before mounting his own horse, and Hendry, along with two other guards, mounted their horses.

He was glad the guards were accompanying them, as he didn't know his way to Inverness, not without the modern roads of the twenty-first century.

It took almost a full day of riding to get to Inverness; they stopped several times to give both themselves and their horses time to rest and to eat. Niall was well aware of the perils of travel in this time—scant roads, the most reliable ones remnants from the times of the Romans, and bandits. To his relief, the ride south was largely uneventful and even relaxing. His gaze kept sliding to Caitria as she rode along at his side, her long auburn hair flowing behind her, a shy smile curving her lips whenever she caught his eyes on her. He could almost forget his dread about what was to come as he focused on the joy on her face, the light in her eyes.

As dusk fell, Inverness came into view, and Niall took it in. Green moors and rolling hills surrounded it on all sides, and he could make out the ruins of a castle on the hill that lay just beyond it. In his time, Inverness Castle would stand on that spot. In this time, the castle that previously stood there had burned down decades before, and wouldn't be rebuilt until the fifteenth century. The River Ness lay just beyond the hill, glittering in the fading sunlight.

When they made their way into Inverness, Niall tried to keep his expression neutral, though it was hard not to stare in amazement at the early version of the city he was familiar with. In this time, it was a bustling market town that consisted of a small port and market, dotted with quaint homes and shops made of wood, some with thatched roofs, and filled with meandering streets of both dirt and cobblestone. It was certainly more pungent than in his time—with the smell of horse manure and fish from the small port wafting in the air.

They arrived at an inn in central Inverness and dismounted, a stable boy rushing out to take their horses. The owner, Lachlan, greeted them with wide smiles; he knew Caitria's father and gave them two of the best private rooms and even arranged for them to dine privately.

"Only the best for Drostan MacGreghor's

daughter and her betrothed," Lachlan said with a smile, leaving them alone to eat a meal of herring, bread and an assortment of roasted vegetables.

"Yer father has many friends," Niall observed with a smile.

"Father is kinder than most of the Highland lairds. He tries tae stay neutral in conflicts and often works tae resolve them. He lent Lachlan money some time back when he ran into troubles," Caitria responded. She set down her knife, leaning back in her chair. "I cannae believe he consented for me tae leave the MacGreghor lands. I never want tae forget this day."

"Ye havenae seen Inverness properly yet," he said with a teasing smile.

"I ken—but I doonae want tae forget a single moment of this trip. I doonae ken if I'll be able tae travel like this again," she said, her smile faltering. But her eyes lit up as she reached across the table to take his hand. "Unless ye keep yer promise and we travel after we wed."

She probed his gaze, as if waiting eagerly for his response, but he couldn't utter the lie. Her smile vanished.

"Artair? Please—if there's something ye need tae tell me—"

"There is," he said, and she looked startled at his stark admission. "But not now. Tomorrow, after ye've had a chance tae explore."

She looked uncertain, but gave him a nod.

"Do ye promise tae tell me tomorrow?" she pressed.

"Aye," he said, savoring the relieved smile that tugged at her lips, the look of utter trust in her eyes as she gazed at him, because after tomorrow, he doubted she would ever look at him the same way again.

THE NEXT DAY was a blur of activity. He played tour guide, drawing on his historical knowledge of Inverness. He first took her to the ruins of the castle on Auld Castlehill, where they took in the waters of the River Ness and a panoramic view of the sprawling village. He pointed out the nearby hill of Craig Phadrig, visible from Inverness, which was the probable site of a Pictish king's settlement and still bore traces of an Iron Age hillfort.

Before they left the hill, he ached to tell her that King Duncan was killed at this castle by a Gaelic king, which inspired William Shakespeare's *Macbeth*—but he held his tongue, as Shakespeare hadn't yet been born.

He then took her to see the old church on St. Michael's Mount, where in his time, a newer church stood—the Old High Church.

As they approached it, he froze, turning to look at the narrow road behind them. He recalled the sense of déjà vu that struck him in his time, when he'd stopped at the stop sign and seen the Old High

Church. It was because he'd been here before, in a different time.

"Artair?" Caitria asked, pulling him from his stunned thoughts. "Are ye all right?"

"Aye," he said, swallowing.

He took her hand and led her closer to the church. From their vantage point, they could see the Dominican Friary—long gone in his time. Niall stared down at it in awe, unable to rein in his historian's awe at seeing buildings that no longer existed in his present. He thought about the déjà vu he'd experienced in the present—did that somehow mean that this trip was predetermined? Was he always destined to come to this time and take Caitria to Inverness?

He had to forcibly push his jumbled thoughts aside, and took Caitria to Inverness's bustling market, filled with merchants, both traveling and local, hawking their wares of wool, fur, and hides.

He'd feared the sights would bore Caitria, but instead she took in everything with a wide-eyed delight that was infectious, stopping to ask him questions every now and then.

When they'd taken in all there was to see—and he could tell that the guards who trailed them from a distance had grown restless—they returned to the inn.

Once they were in her chamber, she pulled him close, standing on her tiptoes to fuse her mouth to his. He held her close as they kissed, breaking apart only when they were both breathless.

"Artair, thank ye," she said. "I've had a wonderful day."

He swallowed and forced a smile. He knew that he had to tell her now . . . there could be no more delay.

"I'm glad," he said. "But . . . I need to tell you something."

She stiffened, her eyes widening. He'd dropped the accent he'd taken on since arriving in this time on purpose.

Caitria swallowed hard, taking a faltering step back. The small movement—a signifier of her growing unease and distrust—splintered his heart. But he forced himself to continue.

"Caitria . . . I'm not Artair. My name is Niall O'Kean."

CHAPTER 12

"Caitria."

Artair's—*Niall's*—voice, seemed to come from far away. Caitria was dimly aware that she had sunk down onto the bed, not looking at the man she'd thought was Artair, her betrothed.

"Caitria, please say something."

She opened her mouth, but no words came. All she could hear was everything he'd told her, swirling around her mind like an endless storm.

From the future. Traveled back through time. Mistaken for Artair. Dreams of you in danger. Ferghas has something to do with the danger you're in.

But she could only focus on one glaring fact. He wasn't Artair. He was an imposter.

"Get out."

The words were faint, spoken barely above a whisper. Out of the corner of her eye, she could see that he paled. He opened his mouth as if to protest, but he turned and left her alone.

Caitria closed her eyes, pressing trembling fingers to her temples. The hot sting of tears burned her eyes; she didn't bother to blink them back. This man—Niall—was an imposter. A man she'd come to desire, to care for.

Shame roiled through her as she thought of all the times she'd kissed him, of her fantasies of making love to him and marrying him. There *was* something different about Artair—he wasn't Artair. Niall was an imposter—an imposter with an impossible story.

He'd told her he was from the future, that he was born in the twentieth century. If she hadn't been so stricken she would have laughed. She didn't know what part of his wild story she should focus on—the fact that he was an imposter, which she believed—or the fact that he was from the future, which she couldn't believe.

Caitria had to grudgingly admit to herself that some part of her knew he wasn't Artair. Hadn't she sensed the difference in him the moment he entered the great hall for the betrothal feast, looking at her as if she were the air he needed to breathe? She recalled the fire that roared to life in her belly at the very sight of him. She'd never felt anything of the sort for the actual Artair.

Artair. A sudden fear seized her at the thought of Artair. Where was he? Perhaps Niall—it was hard for her to even think this new name—had done something to him in order to take his place. Her hand in marriage was prized after all; whoever married her got her family's lands.

But if that were the case, why would he have given up the ruse? He could have kept on fooling her. She recalled the utter conviction in his eyes as he told her his story about being from the future—and that he had no idea where the true Artair was.

Perhaps he's telling the truth, a voice whispered in her mind.

She let out a sharp laugh, wiping away her tears. How could he possibly be telling her the truth about traveling through time when he hadn't been honest about who he was?

And then there was his suspicion about Ferghas—his belief that he may have murdered her brother.

"I've no proof yet, but think of it. It makes sense. If he wants your father's lands, it was just a matter of getting your brother out of the way to marry you. He tried to kill me during the hunt—I didn't want to alarm you then because I couldn't be sure."

She took a deep breath, swallowing as she got to her feet. Ferghas was not a good man; she knew that—but was he a murderer? Tadhg had been thrown from his horse after it was startled by a boar—and speared with his own arrow. But what if Ferghas had been the one to kill him as her brother lay on the ground, injured but alive?

A fierce rage seized her at the thought, and she

closed her eyes. It was too overwhelming to consider at the moment.

All she knew in this moment was what she *should* do. Call for Hendry to have Niall escorted back to the castle under guard, where she would inform her father that he was an imposter. The guards would imprison him, demand to know where the true Artair was, and dole out justice as they saw fit. But as hurt and angry as she was, her stomach twisted at the thought. Her father could be merciful and simply exile him, but other noblemen of the clan weren't so kind. They'd demand that he hang.

The grief that pierced her at the thought nearly sent her to her knees. She couldn't allow that to happen.

She didn't know how long she paced the length of her small room, mulling over what to do next and reeling over his words, but fatigue gradually claimed her, and she curled up on the bed, falling into a dreamless sleep.

When she awoke, she knew it was time to face him. She changed into a fresh gown before stepping out of her room.

She yelped when she almost stumbled over a large heap just outside her door. Niall had been curled up there, sleeping, but he stumbled to his feet when she opened the door.

Her heart clenched at the sight of him. Even through her anger, he still had an effect on her.

"Did—did ye sleep out here?" she asked in disbelief.

"Yes," he said, and it was jarring to hear the change in his accent—his accent from this alleged future. *The accent he put on tae fool ye,* she thought with a surge of anger.

She took a breath to calm herself and stepped aside to let him in. He entered, keeping his distance from her as she closed the door behind her and leaned against it.

"I thought about turning ye in tae my father, and letting him handle ye," she said, after a long pause. He blanched but remained still as she continued, "But as angry as I am, I doonae want tae see ye hang."

Because I care for ye, and I desire ye still, she thought. *Even though I ken it makes me a fool.*

"I want ye tae prove tae me yer story is true," she continued. "If you cannae, I want ye tae go on yer way. I'll make some excuse for ye, and I willnae turn ye in."

He studied her for a long moment; she could practically see him thinking. Or perhaps he was thinking of a clever lie?

Finally, he stepped forward. He took her hands in his, and she wanted to jerk away, but the imploring look in his eyes rendered her still.

"I could give you facts about the future, but even that may not convince you. All I'll say is this—I care about you, Caitria. I think you're a beautiful, passionate and intelligent woman who deserves more out of life than the one you've been born into. I don't regret traveling back in time to help you. So I'm going to ask you for one thing, even though I know I don't deserve it. Give me time to prove that Ferghas is dangerous. You still have a few weeks left until you're supposed to wed Artair. In the meantime, we can stay betrothed to keep Ferghas away from you. Once I get the proof I need, you can present it to your father—and then I disappear. Hopefully your father will then let you choose your own husband, your own path in life. And even if he doesn't, you can choose your own path, Caitria. I want you to know that, no matter what."

His blue eyes held hers, tense and imploring. Caitria considered his words, and a lightness filled her at the possibility he presented. Choosing her own husband. Traveling as much as she wished. Having the freedom she craved.

Without Niall. A sharp pang pierced her at the thought, and she lowered her gaze.

But what was the alternative? If she sent him away, her father would marry her off to Ferghas. She recalled that dark look of fury in his eyes, his bruising grip on her arm, and she shivered.

"No," she said finally, and his face paled, but she continued, "ye willnae be the one tae prove that Ferghas is dangerous. *We* will."

She held his gaze, firm, another spark of anger flaring inside of her at the possibility that Ferghas had committed such an act.

Niall's color returned, and she thought she saw

a flicker of pride in the depths of his eyes.

"We'll maintain the pretense of ye being Artair . . . of us being betrothed," she forced herself to say. "But I will help ye expose Ferghas. And then—and then ye'll go on yer way."

He swallowed, and there was a brief flare of pain in his eyes, but he gave her a nod.

"We still have a little time before we need to return to the castle," he said. "There's—something else I'd like you to see."

Caitria hesitated. She should tell him that they needed to return to the castle at once, that their betrothal was now for show only . . . but she was hungry to see more. And, Niall's admission aside, yesterday had been the best day of her life. Who knew when she would next leave her father's lands to explore?

She nodded her agreement.

THEY RODE EAST FROM INVERNESS, their guards riding close behind them. They'd protested when Niall told them he wanted to take Caitria to see one last sight, but had finally agreed when he'd insisted.

She tried not to look at him as she rode, tried to ignore the emotions of betrayal and anger that swirled in her gut. She could feel Niall's gaze on her as they rode, but kept her gaze firmly on the dusty road ahead.

They stopped when they reached a lone stretch

of a sandy beach. He helped her down from her horse, handing the reins off to a hovering guard. She moved away from his touch, moving toward the shore.

"Where are we?" she asked.

"Moray Firth," he said. "A firth of the North Sea."

For a moment, Caitria forgot all about her anger as she took in the glittering waters that heaved and churned onto the shore with awe. Hadn't she longed to see the ocean, the sea? She imagined boarding a boat and sailing out of the firth and to the sea, then traveling south to the continent.

The heat of Niall's gaze seared her skin. She turned, making certain the guards were some distance away before she spoke.

"What is it like?" she asked tentatively. "In . . . yer time? In the future?"

Hope shone in his eyes as he studied her, as if trying to read her thoughts. She looked away from his probing stare. She wasn't sure what to make of his tale of being from the future, but she couldn't fathom why he'd make up such a story.

"It's hard to explain the modern era in a few words, but I'll try. There are tall buildings, some as tall as small mountains. There are cars—carriages without horses—powered by something called engines."

She listened intently as he described the breadth and size of cities in his time, the robust populations, the "technology" that dominated the future. But her interest piqued when he spoke of lands on the other side of the world.

"There are other lands tae the west?" she breathed.

"Yes," he replied. "Europeans en masse won't discover these lands for another century, but they're there."

He turned and pointed west. Caitria followed his gaze, as if she could see these lands beyond the horizon. She tried to imagine what these lands looked like, and the people who inhabited them.

"People must travel a great deal in yer time," she said, unable to keep the trace of longing out of her tone.

"Yes. For a lot of people it's quite common. Caitria . . ."

She looked up. He gazed at her with urgency.

"Do you believe me?"

She averted her gaze, turning away.

"We should be heading back," she said shortly. "Ye ken my parents will worry."

"Caitria," he repeated, and reached for her hand. Heat spiraled through her at his touch. She wanted to jerk her hand away, but she was unable to, and made herself meet his impassioned eyes. "I had no intention of taking Artair's place when I came to this time, I swear it. People just began to call me his name, and I knew that would make it easier to get to you—to warn you. Did you not suspect anything?"

"I did," she grudgingly agreed. "Ye do bear his likeness. And . . ."

"And?" he pressed.

"Ye look at me . . . differently than he did."

"And how is that?"

His voice had dropped; it was husky, tinged with desire.

The heat that spiraled through her flared into a burning fire as she gazed into the blue depths of his eyes.

"Like . . . ye want me," she whispered.

"I do," he said throatily, pulling her close, and she could feel his heartbeat hammering along with her own. "God, Caitria, never believe my desire for you is a lie."

His eyes fell to her lips, and she wanted nothing more than for him to kiss her, to forget that he wasn't Artair, but an imposter.

But she couldn't. She forced herself to step back and look away.

"That changes nothing," she whispered. "Ye're not Artair. Ye're here tae protect me from danger and nothing more. We should return tae the castle."

CHAPTER 13

*N*iall had become an expert on the subtleties of Caitria's expressions—her strained smiles when she was being polite, the glitter in her eyes when her joy or amusement was genuine.

In her more genuine moments, she was careless and free—laughing with her head thrown back and her mouth opened wide, or a light shining in her eyes when she saw something that fascinated her. She'd only expressed genuine joy during their day of exploration in Inverness.

But once he told her the truth about himself, all that open joy faded, collapsing in on itself like a great mountain crumbling to ashes. Her guard was up once more, yet it was a different sort of armor than the one she'd worn when he first met her. She now treated him as if he were a dangerous animal not to be trusted instead of a polite stranger. He'd prepared himself for her anger, for fury—but not for her coldness. He ached to see her smile, to see the light that shone in her eyes—it was like basking in the sun, and now that it was gone, he was hyper-aware of its absence.

In spite of this, he knew she still desired him. He could tell by the way she looked at him when they stood on the firth, the hunger in her eyes plain. If her desire for him was still there, he could perhaps get her to open up to him again . . . to trust him.

During their journey back to the castle, she didn't spare him a single glance, keeping her gaze trained fixedly ahead. He studied her as they rode; her shoulders stiff, her hands tightly gripping the reins.

As angry as she was with him, he was relieved that she hadn't sent him away. It was within her rights to report him to her guards, and he'd had an escape plan tucked away in the back of his mind had that been the case. The fact that she hadn't gave him even more hope—not only did she desire him; she must care about him as well.

She'd surprised him when she told him she'd work with him against Ferghas, and pride had swept over him. He doubted the tentative woman he'd first met would have made such a suggestion. But as proud as he was of her for her newfound agency, he'd have to make certain she kept her distance from Ferghas. A chill spread through him at the thought of the malice in the other man's eyes.

He'd risk his own life before he allowed her to come to harm at Ferghas's hands.

When they arrived back at MacGreghor Castle, her parents and several servants immediately swarmed them. Caitria dismounted, still not looking at him, as Liusaidh and her maids ushered her inside.

"I take it ye had a fine journey?" Drostan asked, approaching Niall as he dismounted.

"Aye," Niall forced himself to say, giving him a light smile.

She's furious with me. But I'm going to win her trust back.

"I'm glad tae hear it. I ken ye must be tired from yer journey, but there's something I'd like tae discuss with ye," Drostan said, gesturing for Niall to follow him.

For a moment, fear circled through his chest, but he reminded himself that Drostan didn't know he was an imposter—yet. Caitria could still decide to out him to her father.

They reached Drostan's study, and Niall stiffened when he saw Ferghas standing there. Ferghas's mouth tightened with dislike at the sight of him, and Niall gritted his teeth, but gave him a curt nod.

"We've had sightings of an intruder on the grounds," Drostan said grimly. "Two guards have seen him, but when they go after him, he vanishes. I want ye tae keep my daughter close under yer watch—I'm hoping that 'tis nothing, but I wanted ye tae be aware."

The danger is right under your nose, Niall wanted to shout, meeting Ferghas's gaze. His instincts told him that Ferghas was behind this as well, but again, he had no proof.

"Thank ye for telling me," he said instead.

"Did my daughter enjoy Inverness?" Drostan asked.

"Aye," he said, making sure to hold Ferghas's fierce gaze. "Quite."

He left the study with fury racing through his veins. How was he going to get the proof he needed that Ferghas was a murderous snake?

He halted in his tracks as an idea struck him.

He found Latharn by the kitchens, flirting with a pretty kitchen maid who bowed and hurried inside the kitchens at the sight of him. Though he was getting used to people seeing him as Artair, he wasn't used to the reverence reserved for a medieval laird.

Latharn straightened at the sight of him, studying his taut face with concern.

"We need tae speak privately," Niall told him.

Latharn trailed him to his chamber. Niall faced him, deciding to speak without preamble.

"What do ye think of Ferghas?"

Latharn stiffened, and Niall could see his guard instantly go up.

"He's a fine man, beloved by many of the—"

"Latharn," Niall interrupted. "I asked what *ye* thought of him."

Latharn hesitated. "My laird, I doonae ken why—"

"Ye can speak plainly with me. I doonae like him, and I think he's dangerous. I want tae keep him away from Caitria. And I think—" He expelled a breath. "I doonae think Tadhg MacGreghor's death was an accident. I ken he was thrown from his horse, but I doonae think that's what killed him. I think it may have been Ferghas."

Latharn paled, and he swallowed hard, his body going tense.

"I doonae like the man either," Latharn confessed. "I never have. He's always seemed—dark—despite the smile he wears for the nobles. But murder? I doonae ken if—"

"Ye were there in the clearing when he aimed for me—ye took the arrow that was meant for me. I doonae think that was an accident."

All traces of remaining color drained from Latharn's face.

"I—I thought 'twas odd that he missed the boar by such a distance, but I didnae want tae believe that he was aiming for ye."

"He was," Niall said, without hesitation. "I think he wants Caitria for himself and me out of the way. I think he killed Tadhg, the laird's heir, so that he would be the one tae inherit once he wed Caitria."

"What proof do ye have of this, my laird?"

"None yet," Niall said, holding his gaze. "And that's why I need yer help."

～

NIALL DIDN'T SEE Caitria until supper the next night; he suspected she was avoiding him. Though she gave him a polite nod when he sat down at her side, it was jerky and forced, and she barely looked at him throughout the meal, responding to any question he asked with a one-word reply.

At the end of the meal, when she tried to excuse herself, he got to his feet and gently took her arm.

"I'll escort ye back tae yer chamber, my lady," he said, holding her gaze, knowing that the socially well-trained Caitria wouldn't make a scene in the great hall. Her eyes flared, but she gave him a curt nod, allowing him to escort her from the hall.

But instead of escorting her to her chamber, he led her down the corridor toward the courtyard.

"Where are ye—" she began.

"I thought some air might be good for you," he said, keeping his voice low, something he now did when he switched to his natural, modern accent around her. She flinched, and he didn't know if it was at the prospect of spending time alone with him, or the sound of his modern accent—the reminder that he wasn't Artair.

Yet she didn't protest, allowing him to keep his

hand on her arm as they made their way out to the courtyard, then to the grounds beyond.

"I'm having Latharn follow Ferghas," he said, once they were alone. "He told me Ferghas hardly spends time at his own manor—most of the time he's here at the castle. Latharn is friendly with some of the stable boys as well; they'll help. Hopefully we'll discover something by following him."

A look of surprise and then relief flickered across her face, her guardedness seeming to melt away.

"Good. I'm going tae ask my maids if they've noticed anything as well."

"That could be helpful," he said.

She turned to head back inside, but he stopped her, gripping her arm.

"It's a lovely night," he said. "We should enjoy it."

He waited, tense, fully expecting her to protest. Relief coursed through him when she gave him a hesitant nod, and they continued to walk.

"It's something I appreciate about this time," he continued, studying her to gauge her reaction to his words. It was important to him that she believe he was from the future. "How clear the air is. For all the benefits of the future, there are drawbacks as well. Pollution being one thing."

She met his eyes, and there was no anger or disbelief there. Only curiosity.

"Pollution?"

"The technology I told you about—some of it

has produced contaminants. In the larger cities, one has to drive deep into the countryside for fresh air. My father . . . he would sometimes take me to the countryside, away from Edinburgh, in between his conferences or speaking engagements."

"Yer father . . . and the rest of yer family," she said, after a long pause. "Back in Inverness, ye told me they're all time travelers?"

Hope darted through him at her words. She didn't ask her question with skepticism, there was only genuine curiosity in her tone.

He let it all spill out: the tales of his relatives who could travel through time, his father's various travels, the portal village of Tairseach, and even the stiuireadh, who aided travelers through time.

She listened as he spoke, her expression intense and focused. He stopped walking, turning to face her.

"Do ye believe me, Caitria?"

"I'm still angry at ye," she said in response, with a scowl.

"I know," he said. "And I understand why. But—"

"Aye, Niall," she said, and his true name on her lips filled him with joy. "I do. I just—I doonae ken how 'tis possible."

He gave her an understanding nod and a smile. It was a start, a start to getting her to open up to him again. She started to turn away, to keep walking, but he again reached out to stop her.

"You don't know how you change, do you?" he

whispered. "How your eyes sparkle when you're intrigued, how your face lights up when you're happy? I didn't see any of that when I first met you. But that's how you looked the entire time we were in Inverness. I know I came here to protect you—but there's more, Caitria. I like putting joy in your eyes. And I will put it there again. I may not be Artair, but I'll do what I can to make you happy while I'm here."

Her eyes were a storm of conflict, yet when he pulled her close and claimed her mouth in a kiss, she responded.

He held her close, hoping that he was demonstrating the truth of his words, his intentions, his longing for her—all through his kiss.

"I do believe yer betrothed is courting ye," Liusaidh said, giving Caitria a teasing smile over her embroidery.

Caitria flushed, carefully poking her needle through the fabric of her own embroidery.

A fortnight had passed since she and Niall had returned from Inverness, and he seemed determined to win back her trust—by courting her.

Every night after supper in the great hall, he would take her on a walk around the castle grounds. During their walks, he would give her updates about the proof he was attempting to gather about Ferghas. Latharn hadn't been able to find anything amiss from Ferghas's daily habits, and Caitria's maids pleaded ignorance whenever she tried to inquire about him. So their discussions about Ferghas were brief, and he would instead provide her with more details about the time he was from—and about himself. She'd tried reacting with cool disinterest, but that hadn't lasted long. In spite of herself, she cared deeply about him and was still hungry for more knowledge about who he truly was.

She learned that he'd never known his mother, who died when he was young, and he did indeed have a distant relationship with his late father—that had always been the truth. He didn't have many close friends in his time, and mostly spent his time working. He told her with a wry grin that he had more leisure time in this time than he did in his own.

And gradually, she found herself opening up as well. She told him more about the close-knit and warm relationship she'd had with her brother, how much she missed him. She confessed how much she hated the formal suppers her parents insisted that she attend, how confined she felt in the castle.

"I feel I doonae have a choice," she told him one evening, as they strolled throughout the courtyard. "I'm all they have."

"That doesn't mean you have to live your life for them," he returned.

"I ken things are different for lasses in yer time," she said, shaking her head. "I doonae have the means tae part from them. Nor do I want tae."

He didn't push the matter as he took in the rigidity of her expression. But he did begin taking her on rides beyond the castle grounds, a quiet defiance to her father's discomfort with him taking her so far. Drostan finally insisted that they take Hendry with them whenever they left the castle grounds. Hendry, sensing that they wanted to be alone, would keep his distance as they rode their horses throughout the moors that surrounded MacGreghor Castle. A rush of delight raced through her whenever they rode, enjoying the feel of the wind whipping through her hair. She could always sense his eyes on her when they rode, and a blaze of heat would infuse her as he met her eyes with a smile.

If he was trying to melt her armor, the guard she tried to keep up around him—it was working. The walls she'd attempted to erect around her soul had crumbled, and the combined need and desire for him infused her once more.

Now, Caitria met her mother's gaze and gave her a stiff nod.

"Aye," Caitria said simply.

But she lowered her embroidery, biting her lip as she studied Liusaidh, wanting to shout what she was truly thinking. *Artair Dalaigh is actually Niall O'Kean. He's a time traveler from the future, here tae protect me from Ferghas, the clan noble everyone loves and trusts.*

"I can feel yer thoughts shouting at me," Liusaidh said, raising her eyebrows. "What is it?"

Caitria hesitated. She'd meant what she said to Niall; she didn't want to see him imprisoned or hanged. She would keep his secret—even from her mother.

"I ken what it is. Ye've developed feelings for Artair."

Caitria's heart constricted as she met her mother's eyes. Yes, she had, which was why his revelation had hurt so much. And given that he was from another time, he'd soon vanish from her life forever.

"Aye," Caitria whispered, blinking back her tears.

"I could tell it was so," Liusaidh said, beaming. "Everything has seemed so different between the two of ye since the betrothal feast. But why do ye look so morose? Ye're soon tae marry the man ye care for."

Caitria forced a nod and a smile.

"Aye," she repeated, as shards of pain pierced her chest. "I ken."

When Niall came to fetch her later for a walk, he took in her tumultuous expression, and stilled.

"We don't have to walk today if—"

"No," she said. She wanted to spend time with him. She could no longer maintain the veil of coldness around him—nor did she want to. And the very sight of him, in his dark tunic and a green plaid kilt, his intense blue eyes probing hers, made a painful longing twist through her. "I want tae walk with ye."

He gave her one of those smiles that made desire jolt through her like a lightning bolt, and took her hand, leading her out of the castle.

"It may be too soon to ask," he said, after they

walked for a brief stretch in companionable silence. "But have I earned yer trust? Yer forgiveness?"

She stopped walking, turning to face him. She believed that he was from another time—and she believed that he had come here for her. He could have kept up the facade, but he'd chosen to be honest with her—knowing that he could have hung once she told her father.

Niall waited for her response, his body stiff.

"Aye," she said, giving him a small smile. "Ye have."

Relief softened his features, and his body relaxed. He reached out to tuck her close to his side as they continued to walk, and she allowed herself to lean into him.

"Is this truly the first time ye've traveled through time?" she asked.

"Yes," he replied. "I saw the obsession my relatives had for it—it was all-consuming and unhealthy. And traveling too frequently can be dangerous. I think it prematurely killed my father— a healthy man like him shouldn't have had a heart attack. Besides, I liked my own time, and I was determined to stay there."

Her chest tightened at his words, another painful reminder that his time here with her was temporary.

"Until the dreams," she said, looking up at him. "The dreams ye had about me."

"Yes," he said earnestly. "They were so vivid; I knew you had to be real. And you are."

"Where do ye think they came from?"

"I don't know," he said, shaking his head. "Maybe the stiuireadh had something to do with it. I may never know."

A sudden thought occurred to her, and a fierce heat spiraled around her belly.

"In these dreams," she said tentatively, "are we ever . . . intimate?"

He stopped, looking down at her. She stilled, her heart picking up its pace at the look of raw desire in his eyes.

"Yes," he said, with deliberate slowness. "We are."

She swallowed and turned away, abruptly changing the subject; asking if he'd made any progress with gathering proof against Ferghas. His eyes were teasing as he responded, knowing exactly what she was doing, and when she went to sleep that night, it was with images of Niall's naked body entwined with hers.

THE NEXT MORNING, Niall took her riding out to the waterfall he'd taken her to before. They traveled alone, as Hendry wasn't able to come with them—he needed to train several new guards. Niall assured him they wouldn't be gone long, nor would they travel far.

When they entered the patch of forest that

surrounded the waterfall, they were completely alone.

Niall pulled her into his arms as she took in the rushing waters, and she closed her eyes, breathing him in. She wanted to hold on to moments like these for as long as she could.

She turned to face him, and he reached down to touch the side of her face. When he leaned down to kiss her, she didn't resist, clinging to him and returning his kiss with a passionate hunger.

When he pulled back, her veins still hummed with desire. She met his eyes, breathless.

"Niall," she whispered. "Niall . . . I doonae want ye tae stop."

Niall stilled, his blue eyes filling with surprise, then with a fierce hunger.

"Are ye certain?"

"Aye. My whole life, I've always done what was expected of me . . . always done what I thought I should do instead of what I truly wanted. And . . . I want ye, Niall. 'Tis like I told ye before, I think I was always aware that ye werenae Artair. 'Tis ye I care for, Niall. 'Tis ye I desire."

At her words, Niall let out a low growl. He seized her mouth with his, kissing her thoroughly before trailing his lips down to her throat. He lifted her in his arms before lowering her to the cloak they'd spread out on the ground, his gaze hungry on hers as he disrobed her.

For the first time in her life, a man's eyes took in her naked flesh. But he more than just looked at her

—he devoured every inch of her body with his eyes, and moisture crept between her thighs.

"Christ, Caitria," he groaned. "You're so beautiful."

He again claimed her mouth with his, plundering it with his tongue before he disrobed, and a painful ache coiled within her as she traced the muscled hardness of his skin, her hand drifting lower to his cock. He let out a low moan as she stroked it, taking it in its length with awe. A small trickle of uncertainty filled her at the size of him, and she raised her eyes to his.

"I'll be gentle," he whispered, reading her thoughts. "Trust me."

He leaned down, peppering kisses down the line of her throat, to the swell of her breasts. Jolts of fire seared her as he seized one aching nipple with his mouth, suckling it to hardness. She'd never felt such pleasure before, and her cry echoed out in the clearing as he released it, suckling the other nipple into the same aching hardness.

He took his time with her breasts, laving them with his tongue, suckling her nipples, until she was quavering and shaking with need.

Only then did he continue to pepper kisses down her abdomen, to the juncture of her thighs . .

.

"Niall," she gasped, jerking with surprise as his mouth clamped onto her center. "What—what are ye doing?"

"Tasting your sweetness," he replied, and she

cried out as his tongue swirled inside of her. She became lost to the sensations claiming her as he feasted upon her, moaning and whispering of how delicious she tasted.

Soon, the pleasure became too much, and she reached down, burying her hands in his wavy hair as her body began to quiver and shake with the force of her release. The clearing around her dimmed, and she placed her hand on her mouth to stifle a scream.

When she came back to earth, Niall was kissing his way back up her abdomen. She'd overheard her maids whispering about what she'd just experienced—how rare it was for a lass to find her release, and when it seized you, how it made your body quake, how it made you forget your own name.

"I just had a release," she whispered, dazed, and he chuckled.

"Yes," Niall said, grinning down at her, gently kissing the side of her throat, her jaw. "In my time, it's called an orgasm. And I intend to give you many more."

He met her eyes as he positioned himself above her.

"Look at me, Caitria," he whispered. "You're beautiful. The most beautiful woman I've ever seen. Even more lovely than in my dreams. And in those dreams, I've seen your face ripple with pleasure. Heard my name on your lips . . ."

Holding her gaze, he entered her soaked center —slowly—his jaw tight with strain. The pain that pierced her was intense and sharp, and Caitria cried out.

"Look at me, my beauty, my Caitria," he whispered. "The pain will pass. And there will only be pleasure. You have my word."

Her eyes locked with his as he slowly began to move. And he was right, the pain eventually subsided, giving way to a deep, spiraling pleasure that twisted in her belly and threatened to claim her whole. His movements were slow at first, before turning into powerful thrusts, and soon his cries matched her own as they moved together, her legs instinctively wrapping around his. Caitria once again felt those quakes that seized her body, and he cried out, shuddering as he spilled his release inside of her.

Afterward, they lay together, entwined and breathless, before he extricated himself from her, covering them both with his cloak and pulling her close.

"That was even better than I expected," she whispered.

"Oh?" he asked, raising an eyebrow. "I take it you've been thinking about it?"

"Ever since the betrothal feast," she confessed, reaching out to trace the line of his stubbled jaw.

"I've been thinking about it since long before then. Since I've seen you in my dreams," Niall whispered.

"And how was it? In comparison?" she asked teasingly.

"Far better, my beautiful Caitria," he said, his words making her heart soar.

She closed her eyes, resting her face against his broad chest, not wanting to think about the day when this would all end, and Niall would depart from her life forever to return to the time where he truly belonged.

fter they'd returned to the castle and Caitria headed toward her chamber, she couldn't stop smiling. She wondered if anyone could see the difference in her. She certainly felt different—lighter, as if she was made of air. She closed her eyes, recalling the feel of Niall's kisses peppering along the line of her throat, her naked body entwined with his. Her first time had been far better than she'd expected, and it only ignited the flare of desire she felt for him. She wanted more. Much more.

"Ferghas, please—no!"

The panicked voice of Ailsa, one of her chambermaids, jerked her from her blissful thoughts. Ailsa stumbled out of a chamber, her hair and clothes mussed, trailed by a furious-looking Ferghas.

They both froze at the sight of her. Ailsa swallowed and gave Caitria a hasty bow before scurrying past her down the hall. Ferghas's eyes held hers, cold and challenging, before they raked over her body. She pulled her cloak around her, bile filling her throat. Unlike Niall's gaze, which left a trail of heat on her skin, Ferghas's gaze was like shards of ice.

He stepped forward with deliberate slowness before giving her an exaggerated bow.

"My lady," he said, standing so close to her she feared he would touch her, but instead, he walked past her after giving her a dark smile.

Only then did Caitria let out the breath she didn't realize she'd been holding. She clutched the wall, taking several deep breaths. She didn't want to think about what would have happened had she not stumbled upon them.

She suddenly froze; an idea forming in her mind.

"Ye requested me, my lady?"

Ailsa entered her chamber, her gaze respectfully lowered. It was hours later, right before supper, and Caitria had sent for her.

"Aye," Caitria hedged. "Will ye help me prepare for supper?"

"Of course, my lady."

Ailsa closed the door and approached Caitria, but Caitria stepped back before she could help her disrobe. Ailsa raised her startled brown eyes to hers and swallowed; Caitria noticed that she was trembling.

"My—my lady?"

Caitria didn't respond, taking Ailsa's hands with a reassuring smile and leading her to two chairs in the corner of the chamber.

"Ailsa," Caitria said gently, as her trembling increased. "'Tis all right. I only want tae help ye."

"Please doonae tell yer mother about Ferghas," Ailsa whispered. "I—I ken servants arenae supposed tae dally with the nobles."

"I willnae," Caitria promised. "Ailsa, I mean it. I'm not angry with ye. I ken that Ferghas isnae a good man."

Ailsa froze, looking at her with surprise.

"But . . . the laird loves him like a son. Everyone loves him. He—"

"Not me," Caitria interrupted. "I want ye tae tell me what happened in that chamber."

"Please, my lady," Ailsa said, shaking her head. "I cannae lose my post here, I cannae get through the winter withou—"

"You willnae lose yer post here. Ye have my word."

Ailsa still looked uncertain; her eyes filled with anxiety.

"Ailsa, listen tae me. I'm the daughter of Laird MacGreghor, and I will one day run this castle. I'll protect ye. But ye must be honest with me."

Ailsa swallowed hard before she spoke. As

Caitria listened, her entire body went cold, rage coursing through her.

My God, she realized with a chill. *Niall is right about Ferghas.* And she knew in that instance that if Ferghas was capable of what Ailsa was telling her —he was capable of murder.

When Ailsa finished speaking, she looked at Caitria with wide eyes, taking in her taut features with trepidation.

"Are—are ye angry, my lady?" Ailsa whispered.

"Aye," Caitria returned. "But not at ye. Ye may leave."

"But—ye need tae get prepared for supper."

"I can get dressed myself," Caitria said, forcing a kind smile, though anger still roiled through her. "Why don't ye take the rest of the evening for yerself? Go tae yer home and rest."

Ailsa shakily got to her feet, but she still looked uncertain.

"My lady—"

"Yer secret is safe. I'll not let harm come tae ye," Caitria said firmly.

Ailsa gave her a relieved nod, moving to the door. Before she left, she turned to face Caitria.

"Be careful, my lady. Ferghas desires ye, and he's jealous of Artair. Sometimes—" she flushed, a look of shame flitting across her face. "Sometimes, he calls me by yer name while—while he's—"

"Ye doonae need tae say anymore," Caitria whispered, giving her a sympathetic smile, though revulsion clawed its way down her throat.

At supper, she tried to keep up a polite facade. Fortunately, Ferghas wasn't in the great hall—she didn't know if she could keep her composure around him. Despite her attempts at calm, Niall seemed to know something was wrong, his concerned gaze sweeping over her face as she ate.

It was only when Niall escorted her from the hall that she allowed her polite mask to crumble. She gripped his hand, leading him out of the castle to the courtyard.

"What is it, Caitria?" he asked, concerned. "Is it about earlier? Do you regret our lovemaking? I—"

"What? No," she whispered fervently, reaching up to touch the side of his handsome face. "Never."

Niall relaxed, though he still looked concerned. "Then—what is it?"

"Ye were right about Ferghas," she returned. "The jovial face he wears around the clan is a mask. He's a monster."

A dark fury clouded his features.

"What happened?" he growled. "Did he touch you? I'll kill him."

"No," she said quickly, a rush of warmth filling her at his protectiveness. But she made herself continue; this was important. "He forces the maids tae lie with him. If they refuse, he threatens tae tell my father they're stealing—many maids cannae survive without their post here, there's no other work for them. And when he does—take them—he's rough. Dangerously rough. He marks their skin; he makes them bleed. Ailsa said he takes pleasure in it," Caitria spat, fury coursing through her. "Ailsa told me she gave herself tae him tae keep him away from one of the younger maids—a lass of only fifteen."

Niall's face contorted with rage; he clenched his fists at his sides.

"Surely we can tell my father this," she said. "He'll not tolerate such behavior from a clan noble. He'll imprison him—or exile him."

But a look of hesitation flitted across Niall's face.

"I agree that he must be stopped. But do you truly think Ailsa will talk? Or the other maids? You say she fears for her post here—she may also fear for her life. Ferghas is well-liked and ambitious. Do you think he'll let the word of a servant get him imprisoned or exiled?"

Caitria considered this. Her father would believe Ailsa, but to exile a noble from the clan required a consensus among the nobles. If even one disagreed or protested, Ferghas would remain. And he was charming enough to make it seem as if Ailsa was a liar or a jealous lover. If that happened, what would he do in retaliation against Ailsa? She shuddered at the thought.

"We have tae at least keep him away from her— and the other maids," Caitria said, expelling a frustrated sigh. "I'll tell him tae stay away from—"

"No," Niall said sharply. "I meant what I said about staying away from him—especially now."

"What will ye say?"

"Don't worry about it." The words came out as a growl.

Caitria studied him, worry swirling through her chest. As much as she wanted him to spear Ferghas straight through with his sword, he would be punished if he attacked Ferghas without proof.

"Niall, you cannae hurt him. My father will—"

"I won't," Niall bit out. "As much as I want to . . . I won't."

"My wedding tae Artair is only weeks away," she whispered, her heart thudding erratically in her chest. "If we cannae use what he's done tae the maids against him—what if we doonae have the proof we need by then? Ye'll go back tae yer time, and my father will marry me off tae that monster."

"No," Niall said fiercely. "I won't let that happen. I won't go back until I know you're safe . . . you have my word."

CHAPTER 16

"'Tis a fine day for a hunt, aye?" Drostan asked cheerfully, mounting his horse.

"Aye," Niall returned, trying not to glare at Ferghas as he mounted his own horse.

He'd been planning for the perfect time to confront Ferghas; he'd preferred to corner him on his own. But when Drostan asked him to join him and some of the other nobles for a hunt, Niall knew he couldn't refuse. He should have counted on Ferghas being a part of the hunt; the man was a sycophant constantly nipping at Drostan's heels.

Niall eyed Ferghas as he gripped the reins of his horse, icy hatred filling his veins as Ferghas laughed and joked with the other nobles. What would his fellow clansmen do if they knew Ferghas enjoyed forcing the castle maids into his bed and causing them pain for his enjoyment? His hands tightened on his reins at the thought of Ferghas doing such things to his Caitria.

145

"Wait for the hunt," Drostan said with a chuckle, pulling Niall from his dark thoughts. He was studying Niall's stormy expression with amusement. "We'll need any ire ye have for the wild boars during the hunt."

Niall forced himself to laugh. Ferghas met his eyes, and it took everything in Niall's power to not glower at him. Ferghas gave him a cool smile, and Niall fantasized about pummeling the smile off of his face.

Drostan seemed cheerfully unaware of their tension, engaging in light banter with the other nobles as several stable boys readied their horses for the ride. As much as Niall had come to like and respect Drostan, the man did have his shortcomings: his stifling of his daughter—and his complete blindness to men like Ferghas.

When they all finally rode away from the castle, Niall kept his focus on Ferghas, trying to figure out the best way to get him alone—even with the others around.

It was only when they entered the nearby sprawling forest, arriving at a clearing where they tied up their horses, that he got his chance.

Drostan and the other nobles ventured forward, on the trail of a boar that a tracker had spotted, leaving Niall and Ferghas lingering behind.

He realized that Ferghas's lingering was purposeful; he seemed to also want time alone with Niall. Unlike the first days of his arrival in this time, Niall felt no anxiety about this. He welcomed it; a dark pleasure filling him at the thought of smashing Ferghas's face with his fists.

When Ferghas turned toward him with a sneer, Niall was ready. He grabbed Ferghas by the throat, slamming him against a tree. Ferghas's eyes widened with anger—and fear, Niall noted with pleasure—as he leaned in close.

"I heard a nasty rumor about ye," Niall snarled, allowing his rage to flow freely through him as he recalled the fear in Caitria's lovely eyes. "I heard ye like tae frighten lasses in tae yer bed and torture them."

"It seems ye've been hearing lies," Ferghas spat, anger infusing his dark eyes.

"It seems not," Niall returned. "I tell ye this—if ye go near any of the maids—or Caitria—again, ye'll have me tae deal with."

"If ye harm me, Laird MacGreghor will—" Ferghas began.

"I ken how ye value yer reputation," Niall interrupted, making great effort to hold on to his accent through his fury. "I ken ye willnae want whispers about yer 'proclivities' tae circle around the castle. Ye go near any lass at the castle again, I'll make sure such rumors reach the laird's ears. And then ye'll no longer be his favorite."

This threat seemed to reach him. Ferghas stiffened, his eyes scanning Niall's face, as if determining the veracity of his threat.

"Ye can threaten me as much as ye want—but I

think ye're hiding something," Ferghas said finally, and Niall tried not to let his alarm show at his words. "And when I find out what it is, Caitria will be mine."

Niall tightened his grip on Ferghas.

"Ye stay away from my betrothed. Ye doonae even say her name," he spat. "Or I will run ye through with my sword, I doonae care about the consequences."

Pleasure filled him at the genuine fear that shone in Ferghas's eyes before he roughly released him, turning to stalk away.

"Where were ye?" Drostan asked, as Niall and Ferghas joined him and the others. A member of their hunting party had slain a boar, who now lay still and dead before them. "We needed yer help with this boar. The stubborn beast wouldnae go down without a fight."

"I thought I spotted another boar in the other clearing," Niall said, surprised at how easily the lie came. He met Ferghas's gaze, daring him to contradict his words. "Ferghas and I went tae check."

"Aye?" Drostan asked, looking over at Ferghas. "Did ye catch the beast?"

"We didnae get close enough tae catch it," Ferghas ground out.

Niall felt the tension in his shoulders dissipate. Ferghas's acquiescence meant that he took his threat seriously. Good.

Though he still didn't have the proof he needed, a vain man like Ferghas wouldn't risk his reputation. Hopefully the castle maids—and Caitria—were safe from him for now. Now he just had to figure out how to get the bastard punished for what he'd done—and the hell away from Caitria.

And then you can leave. Go back to your time, he told himself, but he felt no joy at the thought . . . only a cold emptiness.

NIALL COULDN'T SLEEP that night, still worried about the threat Ferghas posed to Caitria and the other women in the castle by his very presence. The sooner he could expose him, the better. Latharn was dutifully following Ferghas when he could—he had to eventually discover something.

Frustration surged through him; there had to be more that he could do. But given that he had to be careful not to reveal his true identity, his options were limited. He was the outsider, Ferghas the beloved insider. And he had to remind himself that he was in a different time; the word of a servant girl wouldn't guarantee Ferghas's punishment and exile —if she even agreed to come forward. And he feared that the nobles wouldn't see Ferghas's transgressions as cause to punish him, even if Drostan did. No, he needed something that could guarantee Ferghas's exile.

He stiffened as his chamber door creaked open, forcing him out of his thoughts.

Caitria entered, looking sexy as sin in her underdress as she approached. He'd never considered such garments sensual before he saw Caitria in hers; it clung to every one of her curves like a second skin.

His breath hitched in his throat as a sense of déjà vu seized him. He'd seen this moment in one of his dreams about her.

"What are you doing here?" he whispered, trying to ignore the overwhelming rush of desire that flowed through him. "If someone sees you . . ."

"'Tis the middle of the night. No one's awake," she replied. "I . . . I was worried about ye. Ye seemed preoccupied at supper. And I wanted tae see ye."

There was no mistaking the hunger in her eyes as her gaze raked over him, and he licked his dry lips. Though he'd wanted her ever since he first saw her, and even more so after making love to her, he'd told himself that one time was all he'd ever allow himself. But seeing her before him now, beautiful and seductive, he found himself unable to control his limbs, and he stumbled out of bed, pulling her into his arms.

"I'm not preoccupied now," he whispered, leaning down to kiss her. She returned his kiss, her lips fervent against his, and he held her so tightly he could feel the steady drum of her heartbeat against his chest.

Still kissing her, he swung her up into his arms and carried her to the bed, all rational thought leaving his mind. He groaned his pleasure as he disrobed her, exposing the beautiful curves of her naked body to his hungry gaze.

"Caitria," he whispered. "I want you again."

"I want ye as well," she whispered. "I . . . I ache for ye, Niall."

His heart swelled, and he started to undress, but she reached out to stop him.

"Let me," she whispered shyly, reaching out to slide off his tunic. She sat up to place kisses along the plane of his abdomen, and he hissed in a sharp breath, trembling with desire.

"Yer skin is so fine, so unmarked," she whispered. "Are other men in yer time this unmarked?"

A growl erupted from his throat at her mention of other men, and her eyes widened in innocent surprise. He'd never felt such possessiveness toward a woman before—especially for a woman who didn't truly belong to him.

"Don't talk of other men," he growled, and her look of surprise turned into one of playful mischief.

"Why not?" she teased.

"Because," he said, hissing as her hand reached lower to delicately stroke his cock. "I can't stand the thought of you with anyone else. You may not be mine—not truly—but—"

"I am yers," she returned, her gaze rising to meet his. "For now."

For now. An ache filled him at the words, followed by a wave of powerful longing. If only he'd met her in his time. If only she could be his in truth.

He drew in a sharp, ragged breath as her hand continued to stroke his cock. She looked up at him with concern as a firestorm of heat careened through him at her touch, and she dropped her hand. "Did—did I hurt ye?"

"No," he ground out. "Only the opposite."

Her smile returned, and she again reached out to stroke him, her movements becoming more firm. She sat up, giving him a look that was positively sultry, before leaning down to take him into her mouth.

"Jesus—" he gasped, as she bobbed up and down, and though he knew she was an innocent, another shard of jealousy pierced him over just how good at this she was, and he wondered darkly if she'd done this before. Her tongue licked delicately along his shaft, and she let out a moan of pleasure as she moved up and down on his cock. He trembled, on the verge of exploding, but removed himself from her mouth with a pained groan.

"Was—was I doing something wrong?" she whispered. "I—I've heard the chambermaids say—"

"You were doing all too well. Had you kept going, I would have exploded," he confessed, reaching out to gently press her back down on to the bed. "And I want to feel you, Caitria. I want to feel your beautiful body against mine before I come inside you."

She whimpered with pleasure as he reached down to stroke her moist center. Keeping his gaze trained on hers, he sank into her with a groan. He slowly began to move within her, his thrusts increasing in force until he was pounding her lovely body into the bed, his desire reaching a crescendo as he came with a strangled cry, followed soon after by her own cry of release.

Afterward, he pulled her close, though she tried to get up.

"I need tae return tae my chamber," she whispered.

"Stay. For just a moment," he whispered, a fierce need for her coiling inside him as he buried his face into her hair, which smelled of sweet rosewater.

"I—I was thinking," she whispered tentatively, after he'd held her for several long moments, "that perhaps . . . if we doonae have the proof we need against Ferghas in time for the wedding . . . that we should just wed."

He stiffened, looking at her in surprise.

"What?"

"If we're wed, Ferghas cannae come near me," she said. "Even he wouldnae dare cross the bonds of marriage."

Niall considered her words, his heart thudding wildly in his chest. He allowed himself to imagine wedding Caitria, vowing to be at her side for all time, and a surprising sense of joy coursed through him at the thought, a joy he dashed away. He couldn't wed her while he bore another man's name —it would carry the pretense too far.

"Caitria, we can't," he said gently.

She swallowed and averted her eyes, getting to her feet and slipping back into her underdress.

"Caitria, wait—"

"I shouldnae have suggested such a thing," she whispered, not looking at him. "My apologies. If ye doonae find enough evidence against Ferghas . . . ye should just return tae yer time."

When Caitria awoke the next morning, a rush of embarrassment filled her as she recalled what she'd suggested to Niall last night.

How could she have been foolish enough to suggest that they wed? Niall had his own life in the future, he was just here to help her. And there was still a good chance that the true Artair would appear.

Still, a treacherous part of her fantasized about what it would be like to actually wed Niall, to clasp her hands with his and proclaim herself as his for today, tomorrow, and always.

Her chambermaid Eithne entered, bringing her back to the present.

"Laird Dalaigh is waiting for ye outside yer chamber tae take ye riding," Eithne said with a smile.

"Give the laird my apologies, I'm feeling tired

and cannae ride today," Caitria replied, avoiding Eithne's eyes.

She listened as Eithne informed Niall, and after a moment of hesitation, she heard his footfalls disappear down the corridor.

She told herself that this was for the best. She needed to start distancing herself from him, to prepare herself for his eventual departure. Her face flamed hot at the memory of her wantonness last night, she'd behaved like a whore, taking him in her mouth, crying out his name as she'd writhed beneath him. That wasn't the way a proper woman behaved.

Women are different in his time. He'd told her this during one of their riding trips—how it was common for women in his time to have taken a man —even more than one—to their bed before marriage, and how it would be odd for a woman to wed as a virgin.

How many such women had Niall enjoyed in his bed? Jealousy surged through her, and Caitria clenched her fists at her sides to quell it. This was another reason she needed to keep her distance. She was probably just one of many lovers he'd had —and he'd have many more when he returned to his own time, as handsome as he was.

She pushed aside the jealous thoughts when she went to see her father at midday. Drostan was in his study with the steward, poring over records books. She started to leave, giving him an apologetic smile for the interruption, but he straightened and waved her inside, telling the steward to leave them be.

"Ah, my Caitria," Drostan said, once they were alone, reaching out to give her a warm embrace. "'Tis good tae see ye, my bairn. Yer betrothed has been occupying much of yer time."

A heated flush spread across her cheeks at the memory of her body entwined with Niall's the night before. She gave him a quick nod and straightened, focusing on what she'd come here to discuss.

"I . . . I was hoping I could ask ye something," she said, trying to keep her voice steady, though anxiety raced through her.

"Aye?" Drostan asked, leaning back against his desk with a concerned frown.

She studied him, and for a brief moment considered telling him about Ferghas, but held her tongue. Niall was right; she didn't want to risk word getting back to Ferghas and her maids bearing the consequences of his anger.

"I—I was wondering if . . . if it would be possible tae postpone the wedding."

If she could get the wedding to "Artair" postponed . . . keeping a barrier between her and Niall would be easier.

At her words, the warmth in Drostan's face vanished and his eyes narrowed.

"Why? Is Artair not treating ye—"

"No," she interrupted, "he's been nothing but kind tae me. I just thought that—before the wedding . . . " She crawled through her mind, recalling a term that Niall had told her was common in the future. "I could go on holiday."

She knew this was unlikely, but what better way to gain more distance from Niall? And given that her father had allowed her to go to Inverness, perhaps he'd allow her to travel more.

"Holiday," Drostan echoed, his frown deepening. "What do ye mean?"

"I take a break for awhile. Go . . . exploring. Seeing Inverness made me want tae see more. Perhaps Edinburgh. Or London."

Drostan's expression was now cold and dark. Unease coiled around her, and she continued in a rush, "I'd still get married tae Artair, of course, but first I'd—"

"I shouldnae have allowed ye tae go tae Inverness," Drostan interrupted, scowling. "It put dangerous notions in yer head about traveling. Ye ken 'tis dangerous. And going tae England? There's not a single Sassenach I trust."

"I just thought—"

"I've been lenient with ye as of late because I love ye so and ye've always been obedient. I trust Artair; he'll keep ye safe. He kens not tae take ye out of Scotland again. Ye'll stay close tae MacGreghor Castle where ye belong, where the clan and yer husband can keep ye safe."

With each word, Drostan's voice had risen to an intimidating roar—a tone that had frightened her when she was a bairn. But now it wasn't fear that seized her—it was anger. She wanted to retort that perhaps she could take care of herself, that perhaps danger was everywhere, and keeping her close was no guarantee of her safety.

But before she could muster a reply, her father's expression softened, and he expelled a breath. He reached for her hand, squeezing it.

"Caitria," he whispered. "Ye and yer mother are like air tae me. I've lost one bairn—I cannae bear the thought of anything happening tae ye. Ye must stay close where I can keep ye safe."

Caitria's anger evaporated, though she considered telling him that there was already danger in their midst—Ferghas. But his expression was tired and weary, and he suddenly looked older than his years.

She stepped forward to embrace him before leaving his study with an obedient nod. But one day, she was going to tell her father that she was capable of taking care of herself.

She avoided Niall for the rest of the day by remaining in her chamber, and when it was time for supper, she feigned fatigue. Yet when Ailsa entered her chamber with her meal, a determined-looking Niall trailed her.

Caitria stumbled to her feet, startled.

"He cornered me by the kitchens and insisted on following me here," Ailsa said with an apologetic smile as she set down her meal—a meal for two, Caitria noted with annoyance.

"Are you avoiding me?" Niall asked bluntly, after Ailsa left the chamber.

"No," she lied, taking a seat at the table and focusing on her food. "I've just been tired."

"Caitria." A gentle hand wrapped around her arm, pulling her up from her chair, and she was forced to look at him.

"You're embarrassed about last night."

Caitria flushed; it annoyed her that he knew her so well.

"You shouldn't be," he said gently. "I wanted to tell you—your offer was very tempting. But we have to be practical. The real Artair could show up at any moment. And—and you should be married to someone of your choosing. Someone from this time."

"I ken. It was foolish tae suggest—"

"It wasn't foolish. But if you're worried about the possibility of marrying Ferghas—you won't. I will do everything I can to prevent that. We will get him. I promise you that, Caitria."

Though her heart ached at his words, a sense of relief also filled her—she knew he meant every word. They ate in relative silence, and at the end of the meal, Niall pulled her to her feet, and without preamble, he kissed her. She couldn't fight the need that coursed through her as she returned his kiss, and when he pulled away, he rested his forehead against hers.

"I've half a mind to take you right here," he

whispered. "But your chambermaids might walk in on us."

Caitria couldn't help but smile at the thought of her shocked chambermaids finding them in bed. He lowered his lips to her ear, his voice husky.

"Come to my chamber tonight, my Caitria. I want to taste you again. Every part of you."

Caitria's heart thundered as she met his eyes, her own desire for him scorching her insides. *Ye have tae keep yer distance,* she reminded herself. *He doesnae belong in this time. Ye must protect yer heart.*

But that night, her persistent need for him propelled her out of bed and to his chamber door, even as she scolded herself; even as she urged herself to turn around and return to her chamber.

When he swung open his door, all resistance melted away as he lifted her up into his arms, carrying her to his bed.

Their lovemaking was fierce and heated; he feasted upon her center until she came with a cry, and she straddled him as he thrust up into her, his hands cradling her buttocks, his mouth nestled into the side of her neck as he groaned her name. When she came for a second time, he found his release just after her, pulling her even closer as he gasped out her name.

"Caitria," he whispered reverently, peppering kisses along her throat as he lowered her back to the bed. "I could make love to you for hours, for days . . ."

She smiled, reaching up to trace his handsome features.

"As could I," she whispered. *Because I love ye.*

She didn't know when she'd started to love Niall—perhaps her love for him had begun as soon as he entered the hall for the betrothal feast. Or perhaps when he'd asked her—and truly listened—to what her hopes and dreams were. All she knew now was that she loved him with every part of her being; it was why her futile attempts at staying away from him failed.

But they couldn't be together. He was a man from a time far ahead of her own.

Her heart constricted, and she sat up to dress.

"Where are you going?" Niall asked, his voice a low, seductive rumble as he traced her skin with a fingertip. "We were just getting started . . ."

"I should get back," Caitria whispered.

"Caitria—"

"Good night," she said, looking down at him with a forced smile. "I'll see ye tomorrow. We can go riding."

This seemed to placate him, his handsome features relaxing into a smile as he watched her go.

Her thoughts were a jumble of conflict as she made her way to her chamber, and at first she didn't notice the figure standing in the center of the corridor.

"What has ye out of bed at this hour?"

Caitria halted. Ferghas approached her, his eyes predatory. She realized with dawning horror that he was drunk—his eyes were bloodshot, and she could smell the ale on his breath from where she stood.

What was he doing here? His guest chamber was on the other side of the castle. Was he still harassing the maids? Or was he looking for her?

"Ye werenae returning from yer betrothed's chamber, were ye?" he asked, his eyes flaring with jealousy as he took in her scant underdress.

"'Tis none of yer concern," she snapped, trying not to show her fear as she attempted to step past him.

Ferghas's hand shot out to grab her arm, yanking her hard against his body. Caitria struggled, fear slicing through her, but she was useless against his strength.

"He's had yer body," Ferghas growled, looking down at her with disgust. "The body that should belong tae me alone."

"Let me—"

"I ken yer Artair is hiding something—and I'll soon find out what it is," he snarled, leaning in close. "And when I find out, I'll tell yer father and make certain he hangs for it. Then ye'll be mine."

His eyes were wild, feral, and panic replaced her fear as he gave her a sickening smile.

"I was going tae make our first time pleasurable for ye, but I'm going tae make sure ye bleed from every hole for giving yerself tae him," he hissed. "And then I'll mar that lovely body of yers with my blade and inscribe it with my name, over and over again, until ye beg for mercy. Ye'll never forget who ye belong tae once I have ye in my bed. So enjoy yer brief time with him, *whore*. Ye'll never ken pleasure—or happiness—again, once ye're mine."

He left Caitria in the center of the corridor, pale and trembling in his wake, horror coursing through her veins.

CHAPTER 18

*D*rostan summoned Niall to his study early the next morning. When Niall entered, he noticed with unease that Drostan didn't wear his usual jovial expression—he was looking at him with suspicion.

Niall tensed, fear creeping down his spine. Had he finally gleaned that Niall was an imposter?

"My laird?" Niall asked, hoping that his tone sounded even. "Ye wanted tae see me?"

"Aye," Drostan said, his eyes intent on Niall's. "I've learned something about ye that concerns me greatly."

Niall swallowed hard. He remained rigid, trying to keep his expression neutral.

"Yer wedding tae my daughter approaches; there needs tae be trust between us," Drostan continued, his eyes never leaving Niall's.

"Aye. Of course," Niall said, his heart thundering.

"Remember the intruder I told ye about? The one we found wandering the grounds?"

"Aye."

"Well, we caught him," Drostan said, taking a step closer. "And he told us ye hired him."

Niall was thrown so off-guard by this that he just stared at Drostan in disbelief. He'd been bracing himself for an accusation about his true identity—not for this.

"He didnae tell us why, but he did tell us ye were the one tae put him up tae it," Drostan continued, taking another step toward Niall, "Is this true?"

Niall opened his mouth and closed it again, shaking his head in astonishment. Why would this man tell such a lie?

And then the realization struck him with the force of a thunderbolt. Ferghas.

"No," Niall bit out. "'Tis not true. I've no reason tae hire someone tae intrude on yer property—it doesnae make any sense. I'm already on yer property, soon tae wed yer daughter."

Drostan studied him for several long moments, as if trying to ascertain the truth of his words, before he visibly relaxed.

"That's what I thought," Drostan muttered, shaking his head. "I think 'tis a clan we once had a rivalry with—Clan Ruadh. I think their chieftain wants tae drive a wedge between me and my future son-in-law by casting ye in suspicion."

Niall clenched his fists at his sides; it took great

effort to hold his tongue. His gut instincts told him this was Ferghas's doing—the other man must be desperate to get rid of him.

"Where is this man?" Niall asked tightly. "I'd like tae question him."

"I sent him on his way. Didnae want tae start a clan war by having the man imprisoned here for long. But I warned him not tae trespass on these lands again—or I'll imprison him. I doonae take well tae imposters."

Panic darted through him at Drostan's words, and he struggled to keep his expression calm.

"What will ye do? About this other clan?" Niall asked, swallowing hard.

"Arrange a meeting with the chieftain of Clan Ruadh. See if I can get this sorted out," Drostan said, his face tight with tension.

Another surge of anger flowed through Niall. He knew how turbulent clan relations were during this time. Was this what Ferghas wanted? To start a clan war just to get rid of him?

"I'm sorry tae have troubled ye—tae have even asked," Drostan was saying, giving him an apologetic look. "When Ferghas told me what the man said, I didnae want tae believe him. But I trust ye— and Ferghas—with my life," he continued, smiling before waving him away. "Go—enjoy the day. Take my daughter riding or go walking with her."

Niall gritted his teeth, desperately wanting to share what he knew about Ferghas, but he still had no solid proof, and Drostan adored him.

He left the chamber, glad at the very least that Drostan no longer looked at him with suspicion. *But he should,* a dark voice whispered. *You are an imposter.*

Dread darted through him at the thought of Drostan finding this out. He'd hated the way Drostan had looked at him during those brief moments of suspicion.

Niall expelled a sigh, shaking his head. He'd done too good of a job filling in as Artair—he'd come to care about Artair's future father-in-law, and he was falling for Artair's betrothed.

He halted midstride as soon as the thought struck him. Falling for Caitria? He couldn't be. He cared about her—and he desired her to the point of distraction—but he couldn't allow his feelings to go deeper than that. He would soon return to the time where he belonged and leave her to live her life in peace—and safety. He'd never heard of any time traveler in his family who chose to stay in the past. Scott's sister Isabelle was the first traveler he'd heard of who'd done such a thing.

But . . . for all his aversion to the past, it wasn't as bad as he'd imagined. In fact, he had to grudgingly admit, because he was living as a laird—his life here was probably better than it was in the future. He imagined that Artair had a fine manor in the north, and the guest chamber he stayed in was nearly the size of his penthouse, with a massive bed, a window that provided a stunning view of the surrounding moors, and chambermaids who kept it clean and tended to his every need, even though he constantly assured them he didn't need so much attention. The suppers he ate in the great hall and in the mornings were delicious and varied, from succulent roasted meats to deliciously prepared vegetables and sweet wines and ale, which he'd first found bitter but had now grown accustomed to. And it was truly amazing to live and breathe every day life in the fourteenth century.

He'd also come to have an affinity for Clan MacGreghor. With Ferghas being the glaring exception, he liked all the nobles he'd met, and Drostan seemed to be a fair and kind chieftain.

Even their journey to Inverness had fared better than he'd thought—he'd always thought medieval travel was rife with danger. And while bandits did prowl the roads, it was manageable if traveling by day, or with guards. He imagined venturing to the other great medieval cities of this time with Caitria—London, Prague, Paris, and Siena.

He forced the thoughts aside. What the bloody hell was he thinking? Everyone thought he was Artair; of course he couldn't stay. And if they ever discovered he was an imposter . . . he shuddered at the thought, icy fear traveling through him.

He continued making his way to his chamber, trying not to think of the day when he'd have to leave Caitria behind.

He stilled when he found Caitria waiting for him in his chamber. There were tears in her eyes.

"Caitria?" he asked, panic swirling through him as he moved to her. "What's wrong?"

"Ferghas," she said shakily. "He saw me last night—coming from yer chamber. He threatened me—and ye."

The anger Niall had felt earlier in Drostan's study now flared into full-fledged fury. He let out a low growl of rage, all rational thought vanishing. He'd warned him to stay away from her. He was going to find the bastard and hurt him for threatening her.

"Did he touch you?" he demanded.

"He—he grabbed my arm, and—"

"Stay here," Niall hissed, turning to head out of his chamber, eager to find Ferghas and pummel his face in. But Caitria was instantly at his side, placing a restraining hand on his arm.

"Niall—no—" she gasped. "This is exactly what he wants."

"He threatened you. He put his hands on you," Niall snarled.

"Doonae ye see, this is what he wants!" Caitria cried. "If ye attack him, 'tis all he needs tae tell Father that ye're dangerous—tae send ye away."

Niall hesitated, though his blood still pulsed with fury. *Bloody hell, she's right.* Attacking Ferghas would give the bastard the ammunition he needed to show that he was dangerous and couldn't be trusted to wed Drostan's daughter.

He stepped back from the door, taking several breaths to calm himself.

"The wedding's only a fortnight away," Caitria said, looking at him with a worried frown.

"I know," Niall muttered. "I'll see if I can get your father to postpone it."

"I already tried that—and failed," Caitria said. "I told him I wanted tae travel first. He grew angry with me for the mere suggestion."

"There's a potential clan conflict your father's preoccupied with—one that Ferghas may have inadvertently started," he said, thinking aloud. "If I tell him I want to postpone the wedding until its resolved—on account of your safety—I think he'll agree. It'll give us much-needed time," he continued, and forced himself to say words that twisted his heart. "And you won't have to wed an imposter."

*Y*ou won't have to wed an imposter.

Niall's words kept reverberating throughout her mind for the rest of the day and into the night.

Perhaps I want tae wed ye, she thought with an ache as she drifted off to sleep that night. *Because I love ye, and ye're not an imposter tae me.*

When a smiling Liusaidh entered her chamber the next morning with Ailsa and Eithne, carrying several wedding dresses, it was hard not to flinch. The sight of the dresses was a painful reminder of the facade she and Niall had to maintain. Her mother didn't notice her stiffening posture as she spread out the dresses on the bed.

"Yer wedding day is almost upon us, daughter," Liusaidh said, beaming. "Only a fortnight now. The seamstresses did such a lovely job with these. Which one do ye prefer?"

Caitria looked down at the lovely gowns. How

many times had her mother come into her chamber with dresses for her to choose from? How many times had she forced a smile and chose whichever one her mother preferred?

She looked up at Liusaidh, straightening her shoulders.

"None of them."

Liusaidh froze, her smile faltering.

"What?"

Caitria turned to Ailsa and Eithne, who looked back and forth between her and her mother with open curiosity.

"Please leave us."

They quickly obeyed. Liusaidh was frowning now, her hands on her hips.

"Caitria, what's the meaning of—"

"Artair told me the guards found an intruder on the grounds," she said, evenly meeting her mother's gaze.

"That's for Artair and yer father tae deal with. Ye just need tae focus on—"

"If there's a looming clan conflict, it affects us all. Artair—" she continued, forcing herself to say the false name, "—and I will wed once 'tis resolved. He's talking tae Father today."

"I doonae think postponing the wedding is necessary," Liusaidh said, her frown deepening. "What is this truly about, Caitria? Ye've been so happy, I thought ye were eager tae marry Artair."

"I just want the conflict resolved before we wed," Caitria said shortly.

"Daughter . . . I'm glad that ye've been happier as of late—but ye need tae remember yer place," Liusaidh said, her tone turning cold. "Ye'll be a wife and mother soon. Ye need not concern yerself with clan politics."

A surge of anger roiled through Caitria, and she pulled herself to her full height.

"Perhaps I *will* concern myself with such matters," she returned. "Perhaps I'm not a delicate flower that exists just for ye and Father tae protect."

"What did ye say?" Liusaidh hissed.

"Perhaps I'm more than just an ornament tae put into pretty dresses and marry off tae whichever suitable laird ye and Father choose. Perhaps I can take care of myself."

Liusaidh glared, but Caitria saw the faintest hint of pride in her mother's eyes. But it was quickly gone, her expression turning hard.

"I see that ye must not be feeling well. I'll have the cooks make ye a hot broth. Tomorrow I'll return with these dresses and we'll decide what ye'll wear."

Frustration sluiced through her as her mother stalked out of her chamber. Once again, her mother had dismissed her words. But she felt . . . emboldened now. It felt good to stand up for herself, to voice aloud what she'd silently thought for years.

With a rush of newfound determination, she went to find Hendry, who stood stationed outside the front gates of the castle with another guard.

"Aye, my lady?" he asked, looking at her with surprise as she approached.

"I want a dagger," she said. Never again would she cower before Ferghas if he threatened her. "I want ye tae teach me how tae protect myself using it."

Hendry stiffened, and she prepared herself for his protests, for his dismissal of her demand.

But he surprised her. He smiled and gave her a nod of assent, and she noticed there was a glimmer of pride in his eyes. And unlike her mother, he didn't try to hide it.

"Aye, my lady."

"IF YE'RE APPROACHED from behind, twist back tae take yer attacker by surprise," Hendry said, demonstrating the move.

Hendry had taken her to a forest clearing just off the castle grounds, and had proceeded to show her some easy defensive moves using a dagger he'd given her. Caitria had taken to the lesson well, enjoying the sensation of power that ran through her as she slashed her dagger through the air, defending herself against an invisible attacker. *Ferghas*, she thought darkly. She'd never cower before him again.

"There's my bride tae be."

She whirled to find Niall approaching them, and as always, just the mere sight of him made her breath hitch in her throat. His chestnut hair was windswept, his tunic open at the collar, his blue eyes alight with amusement. Why did he have to be so handsome—and why hadn't Artair's identical appearance not affected her the way Niall's did?

Because ye love him, a voice whispered. *He may be the only man ye'll ever love.*

"I asked the other guards where ye'd gone," Niall continued with a smile. "Should I be jealous of Hendry?"

"I was teaching the lady defensive moves at her request, my laird," Hendry stammered. "I would never dream of—"

"I jest with ye," Niall said, his eyes twinkling. "Please—continue."

She tried to concentrate on practicing, but it was impossible with Niall's intense gaze trained on her every move. There were several times that Hendry had to tell her to focus.

"Ye're off tae a fine start, my lady," Hendry said some time later, lowering his sword. "I do need tae return tae my post. Come find me when ye want another lesson."

"Aye," she said. "I thank ye, Hendry."

Once they were alone, Niall's expression turned serious, his accent shifting to his natural one.

"Your father agreed to postpone the wedding— but only for another week. We'll have no choice but to go to him with what evidence we have before then—and pray that Ferghas doesn't have the means to retaliate. Besides what you've learned from Ailsa, Latharn's discovered a couple of servants who've witnessed or suffered from Ferghas's abuses. As for your brother's death, a noble close to him told Latharn that he acted strangely after Tadhg died—but that's hardly proof of wrongdoing." He sighed, raking his hand through his hair. "I hope that'll be enough to at least cast some suspicion on Ferghas."

She nodded, looking down at her dagger and twirling it around in her hands.

"And then ye'll leave?" she asked quietly, though she already knew the answer. "Tae return tae yer own time?"

He didn't respond for a long moment, and when she finally looked up at him, his face was tight with conflict.

"Caitria," he whispered, "I—I don't belong here."

"Aye. Of course," she said, turning to move past him.

His hand shot out to grip her arm, stopping her before she could leave the clearing. He turned her to face him, his blue eyes filled with frustration.

"You don't know how much I wish things were different," he whispered. "Caitria . . . I ache for you."

Caitria wanted to tell him that she more than ached for him—that she loved him. But she was unable to speak, her eyes locked on his, and when he leaned down to kiss her, she passionately returned it, her dagger slipping to the ground. She couldn't focus on his eventual departure, not now. She only wanted to relish the feel of his hard, muscled body against hers, the demanding pressure of his mouth against hers, the essence of him.

Their kiss intensified, and he walked her backward to a nearby tree, his lips trailing down her neck, to her chest . . .

"I need you, Caitria," he whispered. "You've consumed me, ever since you first came to me in my dreams."

And I love ye, she told him silently, gasping as he lowered her bodice to seize one of her nipples with his mouth, suckling hungrily as he hitched up her gown.

"Niall . . ." she whimpered, as he lifted his kilt, returning his lips to hers.

"Yes, my Caitria," he whispered. "I love the sound of my name on those lovely lips. Say it again."

"Niall," she whispered. "Niall . . ."

His name turned into a moan as he sank into her, hoisting her up by her rear to surge into her. She gasped at the pleasurable sensation of his flesh melding with hers, and wrapped her legs around his waist, her arms looping around his neck as he thrust himself inside her, pounding her into the tree.

"Caitria," he gasped, as they moved together, his breath hot on her face. "My Caitria..."

"My Niall . . . " she returned, his name

becoming a litany on her lips as they continued to move together.

When they cried out their mutual release, she buried her face in his chest, tears stinging her eyes, and despair replaced her sated desire, not knowing how she was going to live without the man she loved once he vanished back through time.

CHAPTER 20

*N*iall escorted Caitria back to her chamber after their hasty lovemaking, regret coursing through him. It wasn't regret over making love to her—it was over *how* he'd made love to her. Caitria deserved worship in a plush bed for hours, not to be taken roughly against a tree.

But wild cries of pleasure had erupted from her lips as he took her, the desire in her eyes hot and fierce, her legs wound around him in a vise-like grip. His virginal Caitria had become quite the seductress, and he found himself hardening against his kilt at the mere memory of her tempting flesh against his.

He looked down at her. Right now she looked like a prim Scottish noblewoman, the only hints of their passionate encounter her slightly mussed hair and the puffiness of her lips that he'd thoroughly kissed. A possessive pride and desire seared his chest as he gazed at her; a part of him had wanted to mark her lovely skin, to show everyone that she belonged to him—Niall O'Kean, not Artair Dalaigh.

But she's not yours. He recalled the strain in her voice when she asked him about his departure. A chasm of grief opened up in his chest at the thought. He missed Caitria when they weren't in the same room, aching for her with a longing that was almost unbearable at times. How would he fare when they were centuries apart?

When they reached her chamber, he reached out and took her hand without thinking. He leaned forward to give the appearance of offering her a mere peck on the cheek in case a servant walked by, but he placed his lips by her ear.

"The next time I make love to you, it will be for hours in a bed. You deserve more than a quick rut against a tree."

A hot flush crept up Caitria's throat, but she evenly held his gaze.

"Perhaps I enjoy a quick rut against a tree."

She entered her chamber before he could respond, leaving him looking after her in open-mouthed astonishment. She had indeed transformed from the innocent woman whose virginity he'd taken. He swallowed hard, desire once again coiling in his belly. It took everything in his power to not follow her into the chamber, to make love to her again as thoroughly as he'd just promised.

He forced himself to turn away and make his

way back to his chamber. He found Latharn waiting outside his door, urgency in his eyes.

"I followed Ferghas today—but I lost his trail," Latharn said, when Niall ushered him inside. "He didnae return tae his manor—it seems he left the lands of the clan altogether."

Niall stilled. He'd learned from Latharn that Ferghas rarely left the lands of Clan MacGreghor, only venturing to and from the castle and his manor.

"If 'tis not a danger tae ye, try tae follow him. See if ye can find out where he's going," Niall said, his heart hammering. "And Latharn—thank ye for doing this."

He'd learned more about Latharn during these past few weeks, gleaning that Artair had hired Latharn when he was in dire need of a post. Latharn was the eldest son of a large family who had a small farm; he sent his earnings home to them—he'd learned that Artair generously sent them more food whenever his family had a bad season. It now made sense to him why Latharn harbored such loyalty to Artair—and why Artair relied upon him. Latharn was a good man.

"I'm glad tae help," Latharn said, his expression darkening. "Ye're not the only one who distrusts Ferghas. No one before ye has dared tae try and gather evidence against him, he's so beloved by the laird. There are many who say Laird MacGreghor looks at him as a son now that his own son has died."

"A son he may have murdered," Niall bit out. He stilled, considering Latharn's words. "If the laird loves Ferghas so much, why didnae he marry Caitria off tae him instead?"

"I doonae ken," Latharn said, as if considering this question for the first time. "Perhaps deep down, the laird suspects all isnae as it seems when it comes tae Ferghas."

After Latharn left, Niall pondered Latharn's observation. He could only hope that Latharn was right, and deep down, Drostan indeed suspected there was something dark about Ferghas.

He rubbed his temples. What in bloody hell was Ferghas up to? He was glad that Drostan had agreed to postpone the wedding, but they still only had a couple of weeks. And then he'd have no choice but to go to Drostan with the scant evidence he had against Ferghas.

And then . . . he'd have to return to his own time.

He closed his eyes against the wave of pain that swept over him at the thought, and when he opened his eyes again, a strange sight pulled him away from his pained thoughts.

He moved closer to his window, staring out. A figure stood on the edge of the castle grounds, just outside the gates . . . watching him. Though the man was far away, there was something familiar about his build, and Niall was certain that the stranger was looking right at him.

He turned to tear out of his chamber. But by

the time he reached the front gates, scanning the grounds that surrounded the castle, the man was gone.

"Laird Dalaigh?" Hendry asked, from behind him. "Is something the—"

"I saw a man standing out here," Niall said, whirling to face him. "Did you see anyone?"

In his haste, he forgot to change his accent. Panic sluiced through him, but Hendry only stiffened briefly before moving into action.

"I'll have the guards search the grounds," Hendry said, moving past him.

Niall watched him go, anxiety spiraling through him as he looked around, unable to shake the feeling that the man—whoever he was—had been looking for him.

WHEN HE CAME to the great hall for supper, unease continued to swirl around in his chest. Was the man the same intruder who'd been spotted before? Was Ferghas the cause? If so, to what end?

He met Ferghas's dark gaze across the hall. Ferghas gave him a twisted smile, raising his cup of ale in a mocking toast.

Niall glared, sliding his gaze away from him to focus on Caitria. Just being in her presence soothed him, and he found himself watching her every move—the delicate way she took her bites, the sparkle in her eyes as she laughed at some jest made by a noble, and those sly, heated looks she gave him. He felt at home at her side, like he belonged . . . though his true place was centuries in the future.

When the musicians began to play, he asked her to dance. They moved to the center of the hall, all eyes on them as they moved together. All the guests faded away as they danced, and something more than desire spiked in his chest. Longing. Need. Joy. How was he ever going to leave this woman, this woman who'd become like the air he needed to breathe?

You have to. Enjoy the time you have with her, he told himself, pulling her into his arms. And he didn't care about the guests watching; he leaned down to kiss her, but a commotion sprang up around them before his lips could meet hers.

A nobleman, Muir, who'd sat next to him while they ate, was now choking. Muir clutched at his throat, stumbling out of his chair and sinking to the floor.

Niall released Caitria and darted over to Muir, and attempted to help clear his airway, turning him over to his side, pounding him on his back. But Muir continued to writhe and gasp until his face went dangerously pale . . . and his body stilled.

CHAPTER 21

Caitria watched, stunned and shaken, as Muir died in Niall's arms. She'd known Muir since she was a bairn; he'd gifted her with books about the faraway lands she'd always dreamed of visiting throughout the years. And now he was dead.

Chaos had erupted around her—some women screamed while other guests were crowding around Muir's body, letting out cries of horror. Her father stumbled to his feet and ordered everyone out of the hall while several male servants rushed forward to carry away Muir's body.

Niall moved back to allow the men to lift Muir's body, his eyes meeting hers. They seemed to share the same thought, and their eyes both strayed to Ferghas, who stood several feet away. He was looking down at Muir without any surprise at all—instead, he looked disappointed and even bored.

Oh God, Caitria thought, ice filling her veins. Ferghas had done this—he'd poisoned Muir, and she had no doubt he intended to kill Niall instead. Her eyes darted to the cup of stew Muir had eaten from. Their cups must have been accidentally switched—which had saved Niall and proven fatal for Muir.

A firm hand gripped her arm, and she dimly realized that Niall was now at her side, his arm around her, guiding her out of the hall. It was only when they were in her chamber that she emerged from her haze of shock, dissolving into tears. Niall held her close, murmuring soothing words as he stroked her hair. When her tears subsided, she backed up, fear coiling around her.

"This—this was Ferghas's doing. I ken it," she whispered.

"I know," Niall gravely agreed.

"That—that poison was meant for ye," she continued, her heart constricting at the thought.

"I know," Niall repeated, his expression dark.

"Ye have tae leave," she whispered, gripping the front of his tunic with wild eyes. She loved him desperately and wanted him to stay with her more than anything—but not at the cost of his life. "Now."

"Caitria—"

"Please—" she said, her voice breaking. Ferghas was a cold-blooded murderer and he seemed determined to kill Niall. "He's already tried tae kill ye—twice. He willnae stop. Ye have tae leave!"

"I told you—I'm not leaving until Ferghas is imprisoned or executed for what he's done. I won't allow him to harm you," he growled.

"I couldnae bear it if anything happened tae ye," Caitria pleaded. "If ye willnae leave, then we have tae go tae my father with what evidence we have."

"It still may not be enough—"

"We doonae have a choice!" she cried. "We cannae allow Ferghas tae harm anyone else."

He studied her, his face a tumult of emotions, before he gave her a sharp nod.

"Tomorrow we'll talk to him, after the commotion from tonight has died down," he said, and her shoulders sank with relief.

He reached out to pull her close, placing a kiss on her forehead. "Get some rest."

But she didn't allow him to release her, clutching onto his arm.

"Can—can ye stay with me tonight? I just—I doonae want tae be alone. I can tell my chambermaids I doonae need them tae prepare me for bed."

"Of course," he murmured, taking her hand and raising it to his lips, infusing her with a rush of much-needed warmth.

After she informed a passing servant to inform her maids not to enter her chamber, they slid into bed—Caitria in her underdress, Niall in just his tunic. And though they'd been naked together before, simply lying with him felt more intimate than making love.

Caitria curled into the heat of his body, comforted by the steady rise and fall of his breaths. She hadn't realized just how much she loved him until now, when he'd come so close to fatal harm. Her mother had once told her love was unselfish, and she realized that she loved him enough to let him go—even if it was centuries away from her—as long as he was alive.

She blinked back tears at the thought of his departure, and Niall misconstrued them, pulling her even closer into the warmth of his arms.

"It will be all right," he murmured.

"Tell me something," she said, blinking back her tears, desperately needing a distraction. "Something I doonae ken about ye."

Niall cocked his head to the side, thinking for a moment.

"When I had the first dream about you . . . I tried looking for you."

"Looking for me? But you didnae ken my name."

"I knew it would be difficult, but I thought that I'd somehow be able to find out who you were. I looked through record books, old portraits and paintings. But none of the images I found came close to you. Soon . . . " he hesitated, a look of embarrassment flickering across his face.

"What?"

"Soon . . . I started to look forward to the dreams. Not because I wanted to see you in danger," he said quickly, "but because I wanted to see . . . *you*. You'd consumed me, Caitria. Even when you were only an image in my dreams."

Her heart softened, but she gave him a chastising smile.

"That wasnae about ye," she said. "Not truly. That was about me."

"It was, my lovely Caitria," he returned "You and I are entwined . . . even centuries apart. Now, sleep."

He kissed her gently, and she placed her head on his broad chest, allowing the steady drum of his heartbeat to draw her into the depths of sleep.

When she awoke the next morning, he'd already left, and though she understood why, disappointment still roiled through her.

She sat up, determined to make certain that he'd keep to his word to go to her father with what they knew about Ferghas.

She dressed before her maids arrived and darted down the corridor to Niall's chamber. He was emerging from it just as she approached, halting at the sight of her.

"We're going tae see my father," she said firmly, raising her chin as if daring him to challenge her.

"I know," he said, giving her a reassuring smile. "I was just coming to fetch you."

Relief coursed through her, and he took her hand as they headed down the corridor.

But her relief and determination shifted to

anxiety. They didn't have much evidence to bring to her father about Ferghas. What if he didn't believe them—and Ferghas could twist their words? Her father loved Ferghas like a son; it wouldn't be easy to convince him that he was a monster.

Caitria forced herself to set aside her fear, recalling the horrible image of Muir dying last night. They had no choice—they had to act now.

As they approached her father's study, one of her father's guards stopped them, his expression cold as he regarded Niall.

"The laird wants tae see ye in the great hall."

Caitria and Niall stiffened, exchanging an uneasy glance. They both started to follow the guard, but he gave her an apologetic look.

"I'm sorry, my lady—yer father wishes tae see him alone."

Her unease spiked into dread, but Caitria held firm, glowering at the guard.

"Artair is tae be my husband," she said. "Anything that concerns him concerns me. I'm coming with him."

The guard looked uncertain, but he turned and continued down the corridor without another word. Her hand squeezed Niall's in a gesture of comfort as they walked; he had gone stiff and pale.

When they entered the great hall, her heart plummeted in her chest. Her father, Ferghas and several other high-ranking nobles sat at the long table—including Latharn. A large bruise marred

Latharn's face, and he looked at them with undeniable panic and fear.

Her father and the nobles trained gazes of hard suspicion on Niall.

They ken he's not Artair, Caitria thought, panicked. *Oh God, no.*

"Caitria, leave us. We have matters we wish tae discuss with yer betrothed alone," Drostan said tightly.

But Caitria remained at Niall's side. She'd never defied her father before, but she wasn't going anywhere.

"I'm staying."

Drostan's eyes flickered to hers with a scowl. She stood her ground, her grip tightening on Niall's hand. The moment stretched as her father glared at her, until his expression shifted, to one of . . . sympathy.

"Very well," he said. "Perhaps 'tis best if ye hear this."

He got to his feet, giving Niall a fierce glare. He nodded at the door, and an elderly man and woman entered, giving Niall polite smiles.

Ferghas stepped forward, his smile icy.

"Tell us, Artair," he said. "Who are these two people?"

Panic coursed through Caitria's veins. She could only guess that they were long-time servants of Artair's—servants Niall didn't know.

"What are their names?" Ferghas repeated, raising his voice.

A long silence stretched, and Drostan's face tightened with rage.

"We have reason tae believe that ye're not Artair Dalaigh, but an imposter," Drostan bit out. "Is that true?"

CHAPTER 22

He'd been waiting for this moment ever since he'd gone along with the pretense that he was Artair Dalaigh. He'd tried to prepare himself for the accusation, for what he'd say, for how he'd defend himself. But now, as he stared at Drostan's hard eyes, all of his carefully planned excuses fell to the wayside.

His gaze slid toward the elderly couple who looked confused at the obvious tension in the hall. It was clear to him that these were long-term loyal servants of Artair Dalaigh—people the true Artair would immediately recognize. He'd been lucky so far—no one besides Latharn who knew Artair well had come to the castle. But then again, he'd never intended to stay here long. He'd been playing with fire by allowing his pretense to last this long.

"Latharn told me some interesting things about ye," Ferghas said with a dark smile, gesturing toward a stricken-looking Latharn.

Niall swallowed hard as he took in Latharn. Ferghas must have captured Latharn when he followed him, and from the look of his face, had beaten him to get answers out of him. Even if Latharn suspected Niall, he knew Latharn wouldn't turn him in of his own volition—especially not to Ferghas. *I'm sorry, Latharn.* He should have never had him follow Ferghas.

"How ye doonae ken things ye should already ken," Ferghas was saying. "How different ye've been these past few weeks. The slight differences in yer voice, yer manner. It made me wonder if ye're truly Artair—or if ye just happen tae resemble him."

"What is the meaning of this?"

Caitria released his hand and stepped forward, glaring at her father and the nobles. A rush of fierce pride filled him at her bravery—though he could see that she was shaking.

"Laird MacGreghor asked Artair a question," Ferghas snapped, his eyes flicking past her to Niall, emphasizing the word "Artair". "If ye are who ye say ye are, ye should ken who these two people are."

"What. Are. Their. Names?" Drostan demanded between clenched teeth, glowering at Niall.

All eyes were on him—and Niall knew he was trapped. There was no getting out of this.

He stepped forward, turning to face Caitria, telegraphing what he was about to do with a look.

Caitria wildly shook her head, a look of panic crossing her face. He forced himself to look away from her and face Drostan, the man he'd come to care for and respect.

"I don't know their names," Niall said, dropping the accent he'd used as a shield. "Because it's true—I'm not Artair. My name is Niall O'Kean."

The nobles let out startled cries of astonishment and dismay; Latharn and the two servants' eyes went wide. Dark triumph darted across Ferghas's face, while Drostan looked stricken.

"Ye may leave," Ferghas said to the two servants. "Thank ye for making the journey here. This imposter will be dealt with."

As a guard led the two shaken servants out, Niall stepped forward.

"But I did it for a reason," he continued, focusing only on Drostan, hoping that he could see the truth in his eyes. "It wasn't my intention to deceive you, I swear it. When people mistook me for Artair, I simply went along with it, because I knew it would help me keep Caitria safe. I came here because I believe Caitria is in danger."

Drostan, who still looked stricken, stiffened at his words, his eyes straying to his daughter with panic.

"Why are we listening tae this imposter's lies?" Ferghas hissed. "Guards, send this man tae the dungeons and—"

"I give the orders," Drostan interrupted, his

gaze still trained on Niall. "What do ye mean, she's in danger?"

"I'm a traveling merchant from the lowlands," he said, deciding to go with his original backstory. "I—I admit to watching Caitria from afar; she's a lovely lass. I soon noticed how Ferghas followed her, how he looked at her—and I grew suspicious. I just wanted to help her. I spoke to the servants—and based on what I learned—I came to believe that Ferghas is a dangerous man."

"Lies!" Ferghas cried, his face contorting with rage. "Ye ken yer deception has been discovered, and now—"

"He's attacked and violated the maids of your castle," Niall interrupted, still focusing only on Drostan. "I don't know if they will come forward, but it's true. And—and I believe Ferghas killed your son during his hunting trip. He—"

The nobles let out cries of outrage and disbelief, and Drostan's face went ashen with shock.

"This is an outrage!" Ferghas bellowed, his hand going to the hilt of his sword. "Laird MacGreghor, I ask yer permission tae execute this man for—"

"Listen tae him!" Caitria pleaded, her eyes wide as she stumbled forward. "Father—Ferghas has threatened me as well. And I believe he murdered Tadhg during his hunting accident—he tried tae do the same tae Niall. And last night, he was the one who poisoned Muir, he wanted tae get tae Niall—"

Ferghas let out a snarl of rage and stepped out from behind the long table toward Niall, his face a mask of fury, but Caitria threw her body before him.

"Father, please!" Caitria cried. "He tells the truth!"

"All lies!" Ferghas snarled. "He has no proof of what he tells ye, my laird. He's admitted tae lusting after yer daughter from afar. The intruder we found on yer lands confessed that this imposter hired him—he was spying for him! And I ken that he's taken yer daughter's innocence—I've seen her come from his chamber in the dead of night. An honorable man wouldnae have done such a thing. He would've come straight tae ye with his suspicions. Instead, he ruined yer daughter—he brings shame and dishonor upon ye. And where is the true Artair? I'm guessing ye murdered him as well."

"I—I don't know where he is," Niall grated out, his eyes straying to Drostan. What he feared was coming to fruition—Ferghas's words were taking root; disgust and rage infused Drostan's expression. "But I—"

"Because ye killed him," Ferghas growled. "My laird, we must take action against this murderous imposter."

"No, Father!" Caitria cried. "Please—Niall speaks the truth!"

The hall filled with silence as Drostan landed a cold and unforgiving stare onto Niall.

"Is it true?" he ground out, still looking at Niall

as he addressed Caitria. "Has he taken yer innocence?"

Caitria flushed hot, but she jutted her chin with determination.

"I gave him my innocence freely," Caitria said. "It was one of the few times I've made a decision for myself."

Drostan let out a snarl of outrage, his eyes feral as his hand went to the hilt of his sword.

"I'm exiling ye from my lands. If I see ye—or if ye dare return—I'll have ye executed on the spot. Now leave before I change my mind and have my men cut ye down."

"Father—no!" Caitria protested, stumbling back to clutch Niall's arm.

"My laird, we cannae let this imposter live—" Ferghas protested.

"My decision has been made," Drostan interrupted, his words a ferocious growl. "Now leave before I have my guards take yer head, imposter."

"I'm going with him!"

Everyone in the hall froze at Caitria's words. Niall turned to her, his mouth dry, as Caitria stepped forward, her face full of defiance as she spoke.

"I ken he's not Artair—and I doonae care," she continued. "He's a good man, and ye're blind tae it. The true monster is Ferghas. I love Niall and I'll not let ye send him away. If ye do, I'll go with him."

Niall stared at her, thunderstruck. She loved

him. Beneath all his horror at what was happening, a small trickle of joy filled him.

"I cannae let him stay. I grant him a kindness by not hanging him, daughter," Drostan bit out.

"Then I'm going with him."

"Ferghas," Drostan said, his mouth tightening. "Restrain my daughter."

"No!" Caitria screamed, and instinctively Niall rushed forward to push her behind him as Ferghas approached.

But all the nobles got to their feet at his action, their hands going to the hilts of their swords. Behind him, two guards entered, ready to intervene.

Niall looked around, gritting his teeth in frustration. He was too outnumbered to take them on.

"Leave," Drostan hissed. "And stay away from my daughter."

Niall met Caitria's beautiful green eyes, filled with tears and pain and longing. If this was the last time he'd see her, he wanted her to know the depths of his feelings for her, something he only realized just now, but had perhaps been true since the moment he'd stepped into the great hall for the betrothal feast.

"I love you," he whispered.

And then he turned on his heel and forced himself to leave, Caitria's howl of pain twisting his heart.

Niall rode away from the castle, his chest heavy with panic and grief. He knew the wise thing to do would be to make his way to Tairseach and get back to his own time. Drostan was furious and clearly trusted Ferghas; Niall had no doubt Drostan would carry out his threat if he returned.

But he couldn't leave the woman he loved behind with that monster. He had to figure out how to get back to her.

He suddenly stilled when he realized that another rider was close behind, trailing him. He subtly reached for the dagger at his side. Had Ferghas followed him? Or had Drostan sent a guard to kill him, not wanting his daughter to know what he planned to do?

The rider was getting closer; Niall knew he wouldn't be able to outride him. He veered his horse to the side, hoping to ride into the forest to buy some time, but the movement was too abrupt, and his horse stumbled, crashing to the ground with a neigh of protest.

Niall scrambled to his feet, his heart hammering, as the rider grew even closer. He clutched his dagger as the rider, whose entire body was cloaked, drew his horse to a stop and dismounted, approaching him.

Niall froze as the man came into view, lowering the hood of his cloak.

Niall's dagger clattered to the ground, his body going ice cold, and he shook his head in dazed disbelief at the familiar features of the man's face, so very much like his own.

"Hello, son," his father said, stopping before him with a weary smile. "Welcome to the fourteenth century."

CHAPTER 23

Caitria was still struggling in Ferghas's grip long after Niall left the great hall, fury and grief overwhelming her.

"Let me go!" she spat to Ferghas. "You're a murderer! A rapist! Father—listen tae me! Niall was only trying tae help! Ferghas is the one who's dangerous!"

"The imposter has twisted the lass's mind," Ferghas hissed, his face tight with such fury that he looked as if he would strike her—but she knew he wouldn't dare, not in front of her father.

"Please Father! He was telling ye the truth!"

For a brief moment Drostan's face filled with conflict, before hardening once more.

"What happened tae my dutiful Caitria? The moment ye learned he was an imposter, ye should have told me."

"I didnae because I believe him. Because I love

him," she cried out on a sob, still trying to fruitlessly free herself from Ferghas's grip. "We only wanted tae bring ye more proof—"

"Of which ye have none, because 'tis all lies!" Ferghas snarled.

His words seemed to convince Drostan, whose face darkened.

"Put my daughter in her chamber—under guard," he snapped, turning away from her, and Ferghas dragged her out of the hall as she continued to writhe and struggle in protest.

As Ferghas dragged her out of the hall and up to her chamber, his lips lowered to her ear.

"I'm going tae get yer Father's permission tae wed ye—and soon. And then I'll beat the obedience back in tae ye, and remove the taint that imposter has put on the body that should have only belonged tae me."

Fury and revulsion coiled through her, and she spat on his face. Ferghas stilled, rage contorting his handsome features, and he slapped her. Caitria cried out in pain as he brought his face very close to hers.

"Listen tae me, ye spoiled little whore," he hissed. "I willnae have a defiant wife. Ye willnae speak tae me in such a way again, or I'll cut yer tongue out."

"I'll never marry ye," Caitria vowed fiercely, glowering at him, her chest heaving. "Ye'll die for what ye've done. I'll make certain of it."

Ferghas's face tightened with fury once more,

and she was certain that he would strike her again. She ached for her dagger, which was hidden in her chamber. She wanted to sink it into this monster's chest.

Ferghas gritted his teeth and continued dragging her toward her chamber, where he hurled her inside, slamming the door behind her.

Caitria clutched her stinging cheek, reeling with rage and grief.

"Niall," she whispered, sinking to the floor, despair winding its way through her chest. Had he gone for good? Had he returned to his own time?

'Tis best if he has, she told herself. *If he tries tae come back for ye, Ferghas will make certain that he's killed.*

She closed her eyes, tears streaming down her face at the memory of Niall's final words to her. *I love you.*

I love ye as well, she silently railed. *I want tae be yers, yer bride in truth.*

She didn't know how long she lay on the floor, tears coursing down her cheeks, her body racking with silent sobs, but at some point the door opened.

She opened her eyes as Liusaidh knelt down by her side, her expression tight with worry.

"Oh, my Caitria," her mother murmured. She reached down to help her stand, leading her to the bed. She gestured to a tray of food on the side table that she'd brought with her. "Ye need tae eat, child."

Caitria didn't respond, closing her eyes. She

needed to get to Niall, to find him if he was still in this time. But how would she find him? Where would he have gone?

"'Tis awful what that imposter has done tae ye," her mother was saying, brushing her hair back from her face. "Using yer innocence and naivety against ye. Playing us all for fools."

"I'm not innocent," Caitria snapped, glaring at her mother. "I love him, and I was aware that he wasnae Artair—I think I was aware from the night of the betrothal feast."

"Oh, my bairn. Of course ye think ye love him—"

"I'm not a bairn!" Caitria cried, crawling out of bed, facing her mother with hot defiance. "I'm a grown woman, capable of making my own decisions about who I love! And just because my brother died doesnae give ye an excuse tae treat me like I'm still a bairn!"

The sympathy vanished from Liusaidh's face, replaced by anger.

"Ye're upset. Ye doonae ken what ye're—"

"I ken I'm capable of more than just running a household and being a wife. I've only done what ye and Father wanted, because I love ye both and I miss Tadhg as well. But I will make my own decisions from now on—I willnae end up like ye! Even if—even if it means no longer bearing the MacGreghor name."

Caitria faced her mother, breathless, her heart

hammering with determination. Her mother's face went white, the anger replaced by hurt, and then another look she couldn't identify.

Say something, Caitria silently pleaded. *Tell me that ye understand. Tell me that for once, ye've listened tae me.*

But her mother's expression went carefully blank, and she stood.

"Yer father was right tae put ye under guard. Now that the imposter is gone, perhaps ye will return tae being my dutiful and obedient Caitria."

Her heart splintered in her chest at her mother's words. Liusaidh turned and left her chamber without a word.

Caitria expelled a sharp breath, swallowing hard. Her outburst had propelled her out of the grief-stricken stupor she'd languished in. She moved to the window, looking out. Dusk had fallen; it would do no good to travel in the dark.

But she knew what she had to do. If Niall was still in this time, she was going to find him. And they would return to take Ferghas down and expose him for the monster he was.

She forced herself to eat the food her mother had brought, knowing she would need her strength. When she poked her head out of her chamber to find an unfamiliar guard standing there, she asked him if Hendry could stand guard tomorrow. The guard looked surprised at her acquiescence and gave her a nod.

Caitria barely slept that night, and when she did, images of Niall filled her dreams.

She awoke just before dawn, changing into a simple gown she wore for riding, taking care to slide her dagger into her bodice. She knew that Hendry would help her—he was loyal to her, and despite Niall's deception, he liked him. Together they could try to discern where Niall had gone—but she needed to get out of this castle. Taking a deep breath, she went to the door and swung it open.

Hendry stood there, but he wasn't alone. Her mother stood next to him, taking in her traveling clothes with wide eyes.

No, Caitria thought desperately, defeat rising in her chest, but what her mother did next took her by surprise.

"Go now, before the rest of the castle wakes," Liusaidh whispered. "I've spoken tae Latharn and Hendry; they ken where Niall is and will travel with ye."

Astonishment rendered Caitria still. She just looked at her mother, dumbfounded.

"Ye were right," Liusaidh said, guilt flickering across her face. "I thought about what ye said— truly thought about it. Our grief has sheltered ye— imprisoned ye. And all this time . . . ye've been such a strong and brave lass," her mother continued, her voice breaking. "Go after Niall. We'll figure out the rest when ye return."

Caitria threw her arms around her mother, tears of relief streaming down her face.

"Thank ye," she whispered.

"Go," her mother said, stepping back with a shaky smile. "Go get the man ye love."

CHAPTER 24

*N*iall watched his father in a daze as he tossed several logs into the fireplace, leaning down to warm his hands.

"Starting fires hasn't changed much over the centuries," Ian observed, giving him an amused grin.

Niall just stared. To stand in the presence of his father, who'd died years ago, filled him with a tumult of shock, disbelief and remnant grief. How was this possible?

He looked around the main room of the cottage his father had taken him to. Ian had told him it belonged to a distant relative whose family had owned it for generations; he and other time-traveling relatives used it during their travels in this region and time period. Niall had no idea such a place existed; he would have come here had he known.

"I imagine," Ian said, straightening and giving him a long look, "that you have many questions."

Niall swallowed as he studied him. His father looked to be in his early forties, which meant he would live for another decade. A wave of grief swept over him, and it was suddenly hard to stand.

His father crossed the room in three long strides, wrapping his arms around him as Niall broke down and wept. Niall wept for the future loss of his father, and for Caitria and the danger she was in—danger he'd failed to avert.

When he calmed, his father led him to a chair, taking the chair opposite him.

"How?" Niall whispered, when he could finally speak. "How are you here? Why?"

"I'm here because of the same thing that I suspect brought you here," Ian replied. "Dreams."

"Dreams?"

"I kept having dreams about you in this time period, dashing away from a castle on a horse—in desperate need of my help. Now, I certainly couldn't ask the Niall of present day about it—the Niall of present day hates time travel. So I did the only thing I could do. I came back here—and I waited."

"How long have you been waiting?"

"About a month or so," Ian said. "I guessed the time period by certain aspects of the dream. But I admit—I was starting to fear you'd never show up, and I was in the wrong time."

Niall froze, recalling the strange figure he'd

seen watching him from the edge of the castle grounds days ago. He'd assumed it was the "intruder" Ferghas had hired.

"You came to the castle," Niall said slowly. "You were the one who was watching me."

"Yes. I wanted to see if you were there—but I wanted you to find me on your own, when you needed my help. I know there's a lot you want to talk to me about—but by the looks of you when I caught up to you, I assume you do need my help?"

Niall nodded, his shock over seeing his father melting away as he thought of Caitria.

Ian listened intently as Niall told him . . . everything. From the dreams he'd had about Caitria, to his entry to the castle and everyone assuming he was Artair, to his and Caitria's attempts to gain proof of Ferghas's misdeeds, to his discovery as an imposter.

"And now . . . Ferghas has her in his clutches. Her father's going to make her marry that monster, I'm certain of it—and my coming here to rescue her has all been for naught."

"You love this woman."

Ian's words were a statement, not a question.

"Yes," Niall said, his voice wavering with emotion. He loved Caitria with every fiber of his being and would do anything to keep her safe.

"Well, then," Ian said. "Let's put some food in you—and get you some rest—then we'll put a plan together to rescue the woman you love."

IT WAS surreal to share a meal with his father. But that was what he was doing, eating a meal of bread and vegetable stew, trying not to stare too much as his father spoke.

"That servant you had helping you—Latharn? I approached him days ago when he left the castle grounds and told him where to find me if you ever needed help. I have a feeling he'll show up soon," Ian said calmly, taking a bite out of his bread.

"I doubt it," Niall said. "I've been outed as an imposter. Latharn probably despises me."

"I don't think that's true," Ian returned, giving him a small smile.

Niall studied him, wondering how he could be so certain.

"Artair Dalaigh," Niall said finally. "He's clearly kin; I look just like him. Do you know of him? Where he is?"

"No," Ian said. "I suspect that he's now in our time—and even if that's so, it's not our concern. There was a similar incident years ago—your cousin Regina went back in time and was mistaken for a relative she resembled. That relative took her place in the present."

"What happened?"

"A stiuireadh resolved it," Ian said. "They both returned to their respective times—with wild stories, I'm sure—but in one piece. I wouldn't worry about Artair Dalaigh—I'm sure a stiuireadh is handling it as we speak."

Niall stared at his father, his heart plummeting in his chest. Did that mean a stiuireadh would return him to his own time?

His father read his thoughts, setting down his bread and leaning back in his chair.

"You want to stay in this time, don't you?"

"I have no choice. My place is with Caitria."

There was no uncertainty in his tone, and it surprised him how good it felt to say the words aloud. He couldn't leave Caitria behind; she was the woman he loved, the beacon that had pulled him back through time to her side. Perhaps his fate was sealed the moment he stepped into the great hall and his eyes locked with hers; fate coming full circle to forever bind him to the woman he loved.

Ian smiled. He stood and clamped his hand on Niall's shoulder.

"Don't worry. A stiuireadh won't force you to leave if you choose to stay in this time. It's getting late," he said, looking out the window at the darkening sky. "You should get some rest. I suspect Latharn will get here tomorrow—hopefully with a reinforcement or two to help us."

Niall knew that he wouldn't be able to sleep, considering that his father, someone he never thought he'd see again, was only a room away—and Caitria was still trapped in the castle with Ferghas. It took great effort to calm the maelstrom of his thoughts and focus on his anchor, his Caitria, and how they could get her away from Ferghas.

When the pounding of horse hooves approached the cottage just after dawn, he was still drifting in and out of sleep. He jerked upright at the sound, reaching for his dagger.

He stumbled out of his bedroom and hurried to the main room of the cottage, where his father was opening the door.

"Dad, be careful," Niall warned.

"Right on time," Ian said, by way of reply, his lips curving in a smile.

Niall reached his father's side by the open door, watching in astonishment as Latharn and Hendry dismounted and approached . . . with Caitria.

Shock spiraled through him at the sight of her. Caitria raced to him, throwing her arms around him as he enveloped her in his arms.

"What are you doing here?" he breathed.

"My mother," Caitria said, shaking her head in amazement. "She helped me flee. Hendry and I found Latharn in the stables . . . he knew where tae find ye."

"I may have had something to do with that," Ian said from behind them.

Caitria stilled as she looked past Niall at his father, and he could see her taking in their obvious resemblance.

"Niall," she whispered. "Who . . .?"

"Caitria," he said, turning back to give his

father a wan smile. "Meet my father . . . Ian O'Kean."

MONTHS AGO, if someone had told Niall that he would one day be seated in a medieval cottage in the Scottish Highlands in the year 1390 with the woman he was dreaming about, his father, and two fourteenth-century Highlanders, putting together a plan to ambush a Highland noble—he would have told that person they were mad.

But that was exactly what was happening. It surprised Niall that Latharn and Hendry weren't furious with him and were helping him at all—but they told him they both loathed Ferghas and believed he'd killed Caitria's brother and Muir—and they were now well aware what he'd done to the castle maids. They wanted Ferghas punished for his crimes.

"Even though ye're not Artair, I can tell ye're a good man and ye care for Lady Caitria," Hendry had said gruffly, clamping him on the shoulder. "Her mother wouldnae have sent her daughter tae ye if that wasnae true."

His father had told Latharn and Hendry a portion of the truth—that he was Niall's father who'd ventured here from Edinburgh to see his son. Ian wisely didn't mention that they were time travelers—their ability was not something they should share freely with those from the past, given the rampant superstition of the time. But Ian had given Niall and Caitria a long look when he told the men his story—aware that Caitria knew they were both travelers. Caitria caught on quickly, giving him a conspiratorial nod.

They'd come up with a simple plan—but if it went wrong, it could backfire terribly.

"Are we decided, then?" his father asked, after they'd gone over their plan a final time, holding everyone's gaze. "We travel to the castle right before dawn tomorrow."

They all nodded their agreement.

Ian grinned, standing up with a friendly smile.

"There's food in the kitchen, and a spare room for the men."

Caitria seemed to sense that he wanted to spend some alone time with his father and gave Niall a soft kiss before trailing after Hendry and Latharn.

"I can tell by the way you look at her—how your eyes light up around her—how much she means to you," Ian said, when they were alone. "It's the way I felt about your mother. She was the love of my life, and when she died . . . I retreated into myself. That's why I wasn't a good father to you."

"Dad—" Niall began, but Ian held up his hand.

"No," he said. "It's true. I know I was distant—but never doubt how much I love you, son. You're as much a love of my life as your mother was. I want you to know that. I knew coming to this time and helping you was one way I could show you."

Niall's chest filled with emotion as his father studied him, his eyes shimmering with tears. He wanted to warn his father about the future, to not take anymore trips, of the fatal toll it would eventually take on his health.

"Dad," he began, his throat dry. "You need to—"

But his father knew him too well, seeming to know what he was about to say.

"I don't need to know what the future holds, son," he said. "At the moment, I'm glad I'm here in the past, with you."

Warmth washed over Niall at his father's words, and he stepped forward to give him a long embrace before leaving to find Caitria. He found her in his guest bedroom.

"How are ye?" she asked, turning to face him. "I ken it must be difficult tae see yer father."

"It is," he admitted. "But I'm glad we have this brief time together. I only wish we'd savored the time we did have."

"I can tell how much he loves ye," she murmured. "I'm glad I got tae meet him."

"Me too," he agreed. "Caitria," he continued, swallowing hard, but this needed to be said. "If the plan fails tomorrow and I'm captured, I want you to get away. Latharn and Hendry will help—"

"What are ye saying?" Caitria asked, her body going rigid.

"I'm saying that I love you, Caitria. And even if

I'm captured tomorrow, I want you to have the life you've always wanted for yourself."

Tears gathered in her lovely eyes, but she shook her head fiercely.

"Ye think I could leave ye behind?"

"Caitria, please listen—"

"No. Ye listen, Niall O'Kean. Ye traveled through time to keep me from danger—the least I can do is stand by yer side. I'll not let ye be imprisoned, and I willnae let Ferghas win. Ye are the man I love, the man I want tae spend my days with—my years with. Never ask me tae leave ye behind. I'll *never* leave ye."

He was speechless, an onslaught of love and pride sweeping over him as he gazed down at her; this fierce, brave woman he loved.

"I love ye, Caitria MacGreghor," he whispered, leaning down to kiss her.

Their kiss deepened, and she wound her fingers through his hair as he pressed her closer, walking her backward to the bed.

He slipped off her traveling gown as they kissed, and she threw her head back with a cry as he dipped his finger into her moist center, stroking her.

"Niall . . . " she whispered.

"Yes, my love," he replied, laying her down on the bed, gently parting her thighs before dipping his tongue into her sweetness.

She moaned, her back arching as he feasted

upon her, keeping his eyes trained on her lovely face as her orgasm claimed her.

It was only then that he disrobed, lifting his body up over hers as she came back down to earth, his eyes devouring her as he sank into her tight flesh.

She let out a soft whimper as he moved within her, locking her arms and legs around him as if to hold him close to her forever, their movements quiet and unhurried, the only sounds in the room the panting of their breath and their soft murmurings of love.

When they both found their release, Niall silenced her cry by claiming her mouth with his own, praying that tomorrow's plan succeeded. And then, if Caitria would have him, he planned to spend the rest of his days showing her just how much he loved her.

It was still dark as they made their way through the silent countryside toward MacGreghor Castle, just before dawn. Niall looked around at his group of unlikely allies—his father, Caitria, Hendry, and Latharn, a rush of gratitude coursing through him. He didn't understand why he'd thought he could do this alone. He needed them—all of them.

His gaze fell onto Caitria, who was staring determinedly ahead, and another surge of pride flowed through him, followed by fear. He didn't want to let her out of his sight once they got to the castle, but their plan of action was a three-pronged approach.

She and Liusaidh would gather maids and any other witnesses willing to speak out against Ferghas. Latharn would work with the guards loyal to Hendry to make certain that Ferghas was imprisoned in his chamber. Niall and Hendry would go to

Drostan's chamber to speak to him directly—and alone—while Ian would wait by the castle gates, ready to whisk Niall back to Tairseach in case the plan went awry. Ian had wanted to join them, but Niall refused—he didn't want his father caught in the crossfire if the plan failed.

Once alone with Drostan, Niall would make a personal appeal to him, followed by the accounts of witnesses Caitria would bring forward. They hoped that without Ferghas's interference, they could present a clear case to Drostan.

It was then up to Drostan what would happen next. Caitria had told him she'd help him escape if their plan didn't work, and he'd agreed, though he knew there was no force on earth that could separate him from her.

His heart picked up its pace as they approached the looming outline of the castle in the distance, and he swallowed hard. It was now or never. Either he failed and ended up with his head severed from his body, or he succeeded and removed Ferghas from Caitria's path forever.

They rode to the forest just outside the castle, where they tied up their horses. Caitria hurried over to him, giving him a fierce embrace.

"Promise me," she whispered. "If this fails—ye'll leave. Ye'll go back tae your own time, where ye'll be safe."

Her voice broke as she looked at him with desperate, pleading eyes.

I'm never leaving you, he thought, but he could

tell that his agreement would give her peace, so he gave her a nod.

She sagged against him in relief, and gave him a brief, searing kiss, before turning to head into the castle—they were heading inside in three separate waves to avoid detection.

He watched her go, his heart hammering. Hendry had assured him that the guards loyal to him wouldn't let Ferghas come near her, but that didn't stop his fear for her.

It was Latharn's turn to leave next. Latharn gave them a firm nod before turning to leave the clearing.

"You can do this, son," Ian said gently, when it was Niall and Hendry's turn to leave. "I'll be right outside if you need to flee. Aren't you glad for all those horse-riding lessons I insisted you take? They come in handy when you're a time traveler."

Niall smiled, though his stomach was in knots. Hendry gestured for him to follow, and with one last look at Ian, Niall pulled his cloak over his head and trailed Hendry to the rear of the castle.

Hendry led Niall in through the rear gates, and Niall followed, his heart pummeling against his ribcage as if it were fighting to get out of his chest. If they were discovered by anyone loyal to Ferghas, Niall knew he was as good as dead.

Hendry seemed well aware of the danger, walking close to him until they reached the winding stairs that led to Drostan's chamber. Niall kept his head down, his hands shaking at his sides as they walked. *Please let this work,* he prayed.

The metallic sound of someone unsheathing a sword made Niall look up, his heart leaping into his throat. A guard he didn't recognize stood at the top of the stairs, glowering at him.

"What is the imposter doing back here?" he snarled.

"He's with me," Hendry said, taking out his own sword. "He may not be Artair . . . but he's a good man and I trust him. He loves the laird's daughter and only wants tae protect her . . . and the laird. Ferghas needs tae answer for his crimes. As head guard of the castle, I order ye tae stand down."

For a tense moment, Niall feared the man wouldn't obey, but he lowered his sword. Hendry stepped forward, placing his hand on the man's arm.

"I thank ye. I ken ye're doing yer duty. Ye have my word that if anything happens tae Laird MacGreghor on my watch, ye may strike me down."

"I could never—" the guard began, shaking his head, but Hendry gave him a firm look. The guard fell silent with a shaky nod.

They continued toward the closed door of Drostan's chamber. Hendry stepped forward, rapping on the door.

"Enter," Drostan replied, his usual jovial tone now sounding weary and drawn.

Hendry gestured for him to enter. Niall took a

deep breath . . . and stepped into Drostan's chamber.

Drostan was standing by the window with his back to the door. He turned as the door opened, no doubt expecting a chambermaid, but froze at the sight of Niall.

Astonishment—then rage—flickered across his features, and he reached for the sword at his side.

Niall made no move to defend himself, holding up his hands in a gesture of submission and sinking to his knees. Drostan approached, his face taut with anger, pressing the blade of his sword to Niall's throat.

"I warned ye, imposter," he hissed.

"I trust him, my laird!" Hendry shouted from behind Niall. "I'm the one who brought him back."

Drostan looked up at Hendry, furious, but Niall spoke up, bringing Drostan's attention back to him.

"You have every right to strike me down. You told me what would happen if I returned, and I returned anyway. I came here to say this: I love your daughter, and I swear on my life that I posed as Artair only to protect her. I know you love Ferghas like a son, but he's a monster—a murderer and a rapist. I think some part of you suspected there was something dark about Ferghas—otherwise, why not marry him off to Caitria? Instead, you chose to marry her off to a benign laird from the north. Because deep down, you don't trust him."

Drostan's face remained tight with outrage, but hesitation flared in his eyes. Niall knew he was starting to reach him.

"As we speak, your daughter is bringing maids and any other servants willing to speak out against him here. We didn't come forward before because we wanted to gather more proof. All I ask is that you listen to everyone's words before making your decision. Do with me what you will, but don't let that monster marry your daughter. Please."

Drostan's face had gone white as he spoke, but he kept the blade pressed to Niall's throat.

"Ye would let me take yer life?" Drostan growled.

"You have every right to. I was an imposter; I betrayed your trust. But I love Caitria with every breath in my body. If you give me your word that you'll not marry her off to Ferghas, that you'll allow her to live the life she wants—I'll happily forfeit my life."

He hoped he sounded braver than he felt. His pulse fluttered wildly at the base of his throat, as Drostan's blade was perilously close to his jugular. But he meant every word he said, holding Drostan's gaze, hoping he could see the sincerity in his eyes.

Uncertainty filled Drostan's eyes, and Niall saw his Adam's apple bob as he swallowed. And just as Drostan lowered his sword, Caitria entered with several maids and her mother.

At the sight of Niall on his knees before her

father, Caitria rushed to his side, helping him to his feet.

"What—what is this?" Drostan asked.

"Servants who will bear witness," Liusaidh said, stepping forward. "My love, they have just told me things I think ye should hear."

Caitria gripped Niall's arm as Drostan gestured for each maid to come forward. Though the women looked fearful, they spoke in great detail of the abuse they'd suffered at Ferghas's hands and their fear of what Ferghas would do to them if they ever came forward. There was even a shaking kitchen maid who confessed to serving the poisoned stew meant for Niall on Ferghas's orders—Ferghas had threatened to kill her if she didn't comply.

As each maid spoke, Drostan's features contorted with a range of emotions: fury, regret, sorrow.

But it was the words of the final maid that changed everything. Her words even surprised Niall.

"He drunkenly confessed tae me that he'd killed yer heir—that he would wed Caitria and what belonged tae ye would belong tae him. And that he would kill ye as well."

The young maid began to weep, pressing her hand to her mouth.

"I'm sorry I didnae come forward, but I thought it was just drunken talk, and he threatened tae—"

"No," Drostan rasped, shaking with rage. "'Tis I who should apologize tae ye. Tae all of ye. As yer laird, I am protector of this castle and all who work and live here. I have failed ye all."

He met Caitria's and Niall's eyes, his gaze lingering on Caitria's, before he turned to Hendry.

"Take me tae Ferghas."

Niall, Caitria, Liusaidh, and Hendry trailed Drostan to Ferghas's guest chamber, where Latharn and two other guards stood outside.

At the sight of Drostan, they immediately stepped aside. Drostan turned, gesturing for his wife and daughter—and to Niall's surprise, him—to enter.

They stepped inside. Ferghas was pacing the length of his chamber, a look of fury in his dark eyes. He stilled, his shoulders sinking in relief at the sight of Drostan, though his expression turned feral at the sight of Niall.

"What is the imposter doing here? Why is he still alive?"

Drostan ignored his question, taking out his sword and grabbing him by the collar of his tunic.

"Did ye murder my son?!" he snarled. "Did ye?"

"My—my laird—" Ferghas stammered, his face going pale, his eyes widening with panic.

"For once, be honest with me, and I may spare yer life," Drostan hissed. "Did ye kill my Tadhg?"

Ferghas swallowed, and Niall could tell that he was trying to think of a way out of this.

"The imposter feeds ye lies—" Ferghas began.

"Answer me!"

"I'm the third son in my family; my father

doesnae ken I exist. Ye've been a father tae me. I should've been born yer son, tae yer family. Tadhg never appreciated what he had—yer love, yer lands. And now ye care for this imposter over—"

"I'll give ye one final chance tae answer or I'll throw ye in the dungeons!" Drostan roared. "Did ye murder my son?"

"It wasnae my intention!" Ferghas cried, his face crumbling, and Niall saw the benign mask he wore fall away. "He—he was thrown from his horse. He—I believed he would've died anyway! As—as he lay there, I realized I could be the son ye deserved, I could—"

Drostan let out a roar of grief and rage. Liusaidh dissolved into tears as Caitria comforted her, looking shaken herself.

Drostan stumbled back, his sword clattering to the ground, swaying on his feet in grief. Ferghas took advantage of Drostan's unhinged state, unsheathing his own sword and lunging toward Drostan.

Niall didn't think—he just reacted. He darted across the room, moving faster than he thought possible, and caught the edge of Ferghas's blade as he lunged toward Drostan.

Niall shoved Drostan to the side, and Ferghas's blade pierced his abdomen. A tidal wave of pain swept over him as he stumbled to his knees, looking down at the front of his tunic that was rapidly becoming soaked with blood.

Caitria screamed as chaos erupted around him.

Caitria was at his side as Hendry and the other guards charged into the room and detained Ferghas.

"Niall," Caitria wept, her eyes wild as she took in his blood-soaked tunic, gathering him in her arms. "Stay with me. Niall, please, stay with me! I love ye . . . I love ye . . ."

He kept his gaze trained on her face, whispering his love for her as the room around him dimmed to black.

CHAPTER 26

"Yer son is as stubborn as a mule," Caitria muttered to Ian, scowling as she closed the door to Niall's guest chamber.

"He's always been that way," Ian said, shaking his head with a chuckle. "He hated being sick, even when he was a boy. I'd have to bribe him to stay in bed. I think he got his stubbornness from his mother."

Caitria warily returned his smile. A week had passed since the confrontation with Ferghas. In the aftermath of Ferghas's attack, the guards had dragged Ferghas away and the castle healer had come to tend to Niall's wound. Fear like she had never known had wound through her as the healer and several servants hurriedly soaked up his bleeding wound with a makeshift cloth tourniquet. After the healer had spent some time tending to Niall, he'd assured them that Niall would recover, as his bleeding had stopped, but he needed to spend a few days in bed resting to fully heal.

The first couple of days after his injury he'd still looked pale, and Caitria insisted on tending to him herself, bringing him meals of bread, hot broth and stew to eat, cleansing his heated skin with a cool cloth, making certain he drank water. Ian had supplied Niall with the pills he'd brought with him from the future to stave off any possibility of infection.

Niall's color had gradually returned, and now he looked more like himself. He kept insisting that he was fine, trying to get out of bed to walk around, though she insisted he still needed to rest.

Caitria met Ian's eyes, rubbing her temples. She'd gotten to spend more time with Ian over the past few days and learned more about him, his travels, his life in the future, and about Niall's childhood.

During their chats, her parents would come to visit Niall; they visited him on a daily basis. When her father first came to visit, tears had shone in his eyes, and he'd thanked him profusely for saving his life and informing him about Ferghas.

"I didnae want tae see who he was," Drostan had whispered. "I miss my Tadhg. I think I just wanted a son in his stead."

"It's all right," Niall had rasped. "You did what you thought was right."

"I want ye tae ken that ye have mine and the clan's forgiveness for posing as Artair. Word has spread about what ye've done, how ye've saved my life and exposed Ferghas. Ye are welcome here, Niall O'Kean."

Joy had spread throughout Caitria at his words, and by the looks her parents gave her before leaving the chamber, she knew they were giving their quiet consent for them to be together as well. Her parents had also welcomed Ian to the castle with open arms, giving him a guest chamber of his own, praising him for having such a brave son.

Ferghas had been imprisoned and sentenced by the clan nobles for assaulting the castle maids, and for the murders of Tadhg and Muir, for which he would hang. They'd also discovered that he'd hired the mystery "intruder," a local villager by the name of Martain, to follow Niall. Caitria had not gone to the sentencing, wanting to stay by Niall's side—and to avoid ever laying eyes on Ferghas again. She'd heard that he'd cursed and railed at Drostan as he sentenced him to death.

As for Artair, Latharn had left the castle to go search for him, and her father had sent out some of his men to scour the countryside. His servants hadn't seen or heard from him since he'd ventured south to the castle—and Niall had inadvertently taken his place.

Ian had told her that it was probable Artair was in the future—but that a stiuireadh would likely guide him back to the time in which he truly belonged. Caitria suspected that when he returned, he would only feel relief at no longer being betrothed to Caitria. Now that she knew what true love and passion felt like, she realized that her and Artair's marriage would have been an unhappy one. *I hope ye find the same love I have, Artair,* she told him silently, wherever he was.

"You should go back in there," Ian said, pulling her from her thoughts as he gestured to Niall's chamber. "My son told me earlier that he has something important to ask you."

Caitria gave him a puzzled frown and turned, opening the door. When she entered, she glowered at Niall.

He was out of bed and standing up, smiling at her.

"Niall O'Kean," she snapped. "I'm running out of patience with ye. Get back in bed—ye need tae rest."

"In a moment," Niall replied, with a teasing smile. "It's just that in my time . . . men like to be on their knees before they do this."

"What are ye—?"

Niall approached, kneeling down before her and taking both her hands.

"I'm staying in this time—if you'll have me," he whispered. "Caitria MacGreghor, I love you with everything I have, and I will love you for the rest of my days. I didn't realize it, but my life didn't truly begin until I had that first dream about you. Will you marry me and become my bride in truth?"

Caitria's eyes filled with tears, her annoyance transforming into pure joy as she gazed down at the man she loved, the man who'd traveled past the boundaries of time to come to her.

"Aye," she whispered. "I'll marry ye, Niall O'Kean."

Niall let out a yelp of joy, standing and pulling her close for a kiss. He reached down to swing her up into his arms. Caitria knew she should protest, that she should insist he put her down and get back into bed, but her overwhelming joy and desire for him rendered her silent.

"I have it on great authority that making love speeds up the healing process," he whispered, as if reading her thoughts, and she laughed as he carried her to the bed.

THEIR WEDDING WAS HELD A FORTNIGHT LATER, after Niall had fully healed from his injury. It was a more intimate ceremony than the one her parents had initially planned; Liusaidh had handed the reins of planning over to her.

"'Tis yer wedding," her mother had said with a smile. "Ye should be the one tae decide how it goes."

Caitria had cut the lists of guests who were to attend and just invited her parents, Niall's father, Latharn, Hendry, and the nobles and servants she'd been close to since she was a girl, including her chambermaids Ailsa and Eithne.

All eyes were on them as she and Niall

clutched hands in the great hall, vowing to love and cherish each other for all of eternity.

"And through time," Niall whispered, just for her ears only, and her heart soared.

After the ceremony, Ian approached, telling them it was time to leave to return to his own time. He gave her and Niall a long embrace, and murmured in her ear, "My son has come a long way to be with you. Take care of him."

"I will," she whispered, tears filling her eyes. Ian turned to give Niall one long, final look before leaving the great hall.

"I think he knew," Niall said quietly, looping his arm around her as they watched his father leave. "He must have known that I would come to this time."

"And I'm glad that ye did," Caitria murmured with a smile.

The day after their wedding, she and Niall mounted her horse Kerr in the courtyard. Her parents watched them from the front doors of the castle, arm in arm. She knew her parents were nervous, but the events of the past few weeks had proven that Caitria was capable of taking care of herself, and that danger was everywhere—it would do no good to keep her sheltered.

She leaned back against Niall's chest as a servant flung their bags onto Kerr's flank. They were heading to Tairseach, and then to Inverness. Niall wanted to send a letter to his friend Scott in the future, informing him that he was remaining in the past, and instructing him what to do with his penthouse and material belongings. In Inverness, he wanted to post a letter Scott had given him to go to Scott's sister Isabelle, a fellow traveler who lived in this time, married to a Highland laird.

After he sent his letters, they'd board a ship at the port that would take them first to London, and then to the continent, where the possibilities for travel were endless.

When they returned, they'd settle into a manor Drostan had given to them as a wedding gift. It would serve as a base for their travels, and where they would eventually have their family. Niall was going to serve as the clan's own personal historian—something her father had bestowed upon Niall at her urging. He'd teach the local children—and anyone who desired—about the past, and preserve what he could about this time for future historians in his own written manuscripts.

Now, Niall gripped Kerr's reins and leaned forward so that his lips were close to her ear.

"After London, where shall we go, wife?" he asked.

"As long as I'm with ye? Everywhere," she replied, turning to him as he smiled.

His grip tightened around her waist, and she gave her parents a wave of farewell as they rode out of the courtyard and past the castle gates, toward their shared future.

CHAPTER 27

Present Day
Scottish Highlands

Diana rolled down the car window, turning up the volume of the radio, bopping her head along to the upbeat pop song that blared through the speakers. She breathed in the fresh air of the Highlands, basking in the view of rolling green hills and blue skies that surrounded her. God, she needed this. Time away from the hustle and bustle of London and her job there as a solicitor. She was spending a long weekend at her family's ancestral home, tucked away amid the lush greenery of the Highlands; she'd been looking forward to this mini holiday for weeks.

She glanced down at her cell phone, tossed casually onto the passenger seat, glad that cell phone reception was spotty here. Her Aunt Kensa

243

had been trying to reach her for the past few weeks, sending her texts and calls that she'd ignored. Kensa was a member of the family who fully embraced her status as a stiuireadh—a druid witch who guided travelers through time.

Diana had long ago determined that she would play no part in magic or time travel, despite having a strong affinity for such magic, given that both her parents had been powerful stiuireadh. Instead, Diana had picked the most grounded, nonmagical profession she could find—the law. Kensa had tried to dissuade her from her chosen nonmagical path, insisting that she had one of the most powerful affinities for time travel in their line.

"I don't care," Diana had said. "I want nothing to do with all that."

And Kensa had to know why, given what had happened to her parents. But it looked like her aunt was again not respecting her boundaries, given how much she'd tried to contact her these past few weeks.

Kensa lived somewhere in the Highlands—likely because it was the location of Tairseach, a portal that travelers and the stiuireadh used to travel through time—but Kensa didn't know she was in the region. Diana had told her assistant to inform Kensa she'd gone to the States on business if she called the office.

Diana soon pulled up to the rambling old home she'd been slowly renovating over the years, taking it in. It was originally built in the twelfth century, its stone walls crumbling, its windows cracked with age, but Diana knew that she could bring it back to a state of beauty.

She got out of her car, slinging her bag over her shoulder and heading to the front door, humming as she unlocked it and stepped inside.

Diana froze as soon as she opened the door, her bag slipping to the ground.

Kensa stood in the foyer and gave her a pleasant smile.

"Hello, Diana."

Diana gritted her teeth. She'd underestimated her aunt's determination to reach her. She must have used her magic to determine where she was—a Locator spell.

"If this is about magic or time travel—" Diana began, through gritted teeth.

"It is." The look Kensa gave her was apologetic —slightly. "But it's urgent. I just helped a man from the present get to his soul mate in the past—Niall O'Kean. But there was a mishap."

"Kensa, I—"

Kensa continued in a rush. "His ancestor, Artair Dalaigh, to whom he bears a likeness—got transported to this time. But he doesn't belong here. I need your help, Diana. I need you to get him back to the time he belongs . . . to the fourteenth century."

～

*B*UY *Artair's Temptress (Highlander Fate Book 5) now.*

246

*B*UY *Artair's Temptress (Highlander Fate Book 5) now.*

Highlander Fate Series

Eadan's Vow

Ronan's Captive

Ciaran's Bond

Niall's Bride

Artair's Temptress

Latharn's Destiny

Highlander Fate Omnibus Books 1-3

Highlander Fate, Lairds of the Isles Series

Gawen's Claim

Bhaltair's Pledge

Domhnall's Honor

Stella Knight writes time travel romance and historical romance novels. She enjoys transporting readers to different times and places with vivid, nuanced heroes and heroines.

She resides in sunny southern California with her own swoon-worthy hero and her collection of too many books and board games. She's been writing for as long as she can remember, and when not writing, she can be found traveling to new locales, diving into a new book, or watching her favorite film or documentary. She loves romance, history, mystery, and adventure, all of which you'll find in her books.

Stay in touch!
stellaknightbooks.com